BOUND FOR FREEDOM

Weekly Reader Children's Book Club presents

Bound for Freedom

BY RUTH CHESSMAN

ILLUSTRATED BY ANNE LINTON

Abelard - Schuman

London New York Toronto

LONDON	NEW YORK	TORONTO
Abelard-Schuman	Abelard-Schuman	Abelard-Schuman
Limited	Limited	Canada Limited
8 King St. WC2	6 West 57th St.	896 Queen St. W.

Printed in the United States of America

Contents

BOUND FOR FREEDOM

Chapter 1

Farewell to Home

James Porter rose at dawn of the morning that, unknown to him, was to be his last in London. He awakened with little to cheer him. It was a cold day in January in the year 1703. The few glimmers of light that poked through the chinks in the barn walls were bleak and drear. Besides he had no right to be here. If the owner of the empty barn came back unexpectedly there would be real trouble.

James was twelve years old, motherless, somewhat small for his age. He looked even smaller than he was because his clothes were all too large for him. At this moment of his awakening, he was chilled to the bone. Yesterday his father had forced open the side door of the barn; otherwise they would have had to sleep in the

9

freezing outdoors. James was grateful for the slight shelter of the gloomy building, although he knew his father
had not thought of him at all. No real provision was
ever made for James. Wherever his father went James
simply tagged along like a neglected dog.

He pushed open the door a little, and saw with a
sinking heart that it had snowed during the night. A
light blanket of white lay over everything. He backed
into the barn again and looked around warily to see if
perhaps after all his father had come in while he slept.
Really he knew better. If his father had been there, there
would have been noise and a beating at the very least.
His father's absence was usually more to be wished for
than his presence. All James ever had from his father were
cuffs and curses. Yet at this moment he would have felt
safer to have him here. Right now he would have given
the world to hear that rough voice. It was so gloomy
inside, so cold and uninviting outdoors. He was hungry
and with no way of finding food. He was afraid, with
no idea of what he should do.

The sun was dawning red, and James took heart a
little. After testing the snow against his thinly shod feet,
he thought he would be able to bear the cold after all,
although he was hardly dressed for such weather. His
breeches had lost their buckles long ago, and instead of
being firmly secured below his knees they hung loosely
to his ankles. They were much too large in the waist,
and he had to make a clumsy knot in them to hold them
in place. He had no jacket, only a kind of smock that

hung gracelessly on his thin shoulders. Still he was used to no better, so he hardened himself and stepped out.

For a moment longer he hesitated. The barn he had just left gave some little shelter after all. Was he wise to leave it? This barn belonged to the great house of a nobleman, and both house and barn were empty of their proper occupants. His father had said sarcastically that it was a shame not to make use of the barn while his lordship was away. James, who knew his father was doing wrong in forcing the door, stood now in great dread of being discovered. If he were caught he would be hanged, for trespass was a serious matter. Yes, he would be safer away from it. Fear gave sudden wings to his feet. He darted over the empty field to the safety of the road, where anyone had a right to walk.

The morning was so new and so cold that nobody was abroad as yet. James, in his thin rags, was so relieved to be off the nobleman's grounds that for a while he was even grateful to the weather that kept the roads free of those who might have seen him. As he walked by one silent cottage after another, however, he began to shiver, and his toes to tingle. He was hugging himself helplessly by the time he reached an innyard.

This was a part of London foreign to him. His father made no settled home, but ran from one place to another as his misdeeds chased him. James approached the inn with a little courage, for in his years of fending for himself he had found that stablemen were likely to be kind.

He went very close to the stables, hoping for a crust of bread and a place in the steamy warmth near the horses. He could hear a horse whinny, and another answer, but the door was shut tight against the bitter cold. He guessed the stableman must still be asleep. James was of a shy and unassuming disposition and did not dare try to make sure.

For a while he stood numbly looking at the stable door, hoping it would open. A brisk wind blew up all at once, to add to his misery. On the breeze came a delectable smell from the inn itself. Early as it was, the kitchen was full of the sounds of activity. A fatalistic desperation overcame his usual timidity, and he went to stand before the kitchen door. After a long time he gathered enough courage to give a light knock. Once more he stood motionless, aghast at his own boldness.

"Here now, what's this?" called out the man who opened to his knock. He pulled James into the kitchen, and James stood dumbly, shrinking and shivering. "Come in, come in, you'll have winter in the kitchen if I don't shut the door."

James stood gaping, his ready-made speech dying on his tongue. All he could do was gasp out, "Please, sir!"

A woman who had been standing by the hearth joined the man, and a plump, good-natured pair they made.

"You've come to breakfast, have you?" the woman asked, and the man smiled and added, "We have an early guest, Molly."

With no more than that James was sat down at the

table with them, and a meal was set before him along with their own. They always ate early to be free for the guests, they explained, and were glad of his company.

"And boy, if you wish, come each morning. You can make yourself useful in the kitchen to pay for your food."

As he ate such a meal as he never remembered having in his life, James thought he must be in heaven. He had never tasted eggs before, although he had heard of them. And with the delectable eggs was a mutton chop. He had chewed mutton bones before, but a whole chop, with meat on it, had never come his way. And the bread! He had smelled it fresh like this while he stood outside a bakery. To find it even tastier than its smells promised was like having a dream come better than true. He ate, and he drank the ale they poured for him, and then he ate again. When finally he said regretfully, "I have no more room," they laughed at him very kindly and promised, "There are other meals to come."

He was very sleepy now from the unaccustomed food and the delicious warmth in the room; but his conscience egged him on, and after a giant yawn he said, "Now I must work to pay for my food."

"And indeed you shall," said Molly. "But later. Now you shall sit by the fire, and tonight if you wish you may sleep near it. Then in the morning you will begin your work."

Gratefully he sat down on the floor with his back hard against the warm bricks of the huge fireplace. In a min-

ute the clang of Molly's cookware as she began the inn
breakfast and the brisk noises of her waiter husband
all ran together and seemed to soften into a murmur.
If only this kind of comfort could be his forever, he
wished drowsily. And maybe it could, if he were allowed to stay here and work for his keep! He could only
hope his father would not in some way interfere. But
why should I think that, James wondered. He only wants
to get rid of me. He calls me a nuisance.

His father! Sadness swept over him to have to call
such a man *father*. He was a cruel, selfish man who
never thought of James as a son, but only as a misfor-
tune. He thought nothing of leaving James alone as he
had last night, with no warning. He had declared his
intention of making the nobleman's barn his home for
what was left of the winter, but during the day he happened to fall in with some new ruffians who, as usual,
instantly became his closest friends. Since then James had
seen no more of him. He had vanished, as he often did,
leaving James alone in the great, empty barn.

"It is so cold here," James had said to his father when
they first entered the barn. "My clothes are too thin."

"What can you expect?" his father said. "If you are
determined to be undersized I can find no clothes for
you."

His father was a tall man and never left off jeering at
James's size. Because his father stole all their clothes —
stole all their everything, in fact — James had not been
breeched until he was a great boy almost seven, his fa-

ther insisting he could not come by a pair of breeches
that small.

"But I am not so very little," James had protested in
great shame at having to wear skirts like a baby.

"You are too small for all the breeches that come my
way," his father roared. But finally he brought home a
pair that almost fit, and James had one of his rare tastes
of joy as he belatedly left babyhood behind.

The clothes he now wore were new to him in the last
month or so, his others having fallen to pieces. His father had not troubled himself about warmth. He gave
him only what clothes and food he came by easily and
conveniently. He was a harsh man, brutal to James.

But he's not here now, James suddenly told himself
through the dreamy warmth. This thought enabled him
to relax, and he dropped into a fast sleep. He slept sitting there, in the first real comfort he had felt since winter settled in.

He was awakened by the rough boom of his father's
voice, although the first words he understood were Molly's, saying protestingly, "Ah, poor lad! Let him be.
He's only been asleep a minute or two."

"Sleep, is it?" his father bellowed, dragging him to
his feet. "Come now, there's not a second to waste." In
another breath they were out in the cold, heedless of
the protests of Molly and her husband.

"Thought to hide from me, did you?" his father asked,
dragging him along with three of James's steps needed
to make one of his.

"No, sir," James gasped.

"No, sir," his father mimicked. "Your tracks led me. Fool! There in the snow lay the story for me to read. Thought you'd hide from me, did you?"

There was no use denying any longer, and in any case James had no breath for it. His father was almost running, and James had all he could do to keep up with him. He was breathing in great gulps of air now and began to recognize the salty, tarry smell of the docks. His father slowed down a little, as though unable to maintain the pace himself, and said with satisfaction, "Thought you'd outwitted me, did you? Eh?"

James couldn't even manage the "No, sir" he wanted to say, but his father went on anyway. "The tide isn't full yet, and I'm saved."

In another instant the wharves sprang into view, with ships creaking against the timbers, with men hallooing and shouting, horses clattering over the planking, cart wheels rattling.

"There she is, a pretty little vessel for a pretty little boy," his father sneered and began to run again, still dragging James after him. Before he realized what his father was about, they were up the gangplank and on the deck of the nearest ship.

"You see, I'm just in time, Captain Foster," his father said, with the hearty joviality he reserved for strangers.

The captain, a heavyset man with no pleasant look to him, said contemptuously, "You're late. Where's the boy?"

"Here he is. Step forward, lad," said his father, pushing James so enthusiastically that he tripped and fell at the captain's feet.

"This boy is never twelve," said the captain sharply as James picked himself up and shrank back to his father.

"Oh, sir, I'm just twelve, sir," James gasped out, feeling a need to make an honest man of his father for once. "Indeed, sir, I'm full twelve!"

The captain stared at him, then turned back to his father. "I've got me a boy since talking to you," he said.

"Oh, but not such a boy as this! *So* humble! *So* duti-
ful! *So* willing!"

Each time his father said the word "so" he pushed
James toward the captain with a sharp poke of his finger in the small of James's back. At the end James was
again very close to the captain, who looked at him doubtfully, then said to his father, "I'll never give you two
pounds for him."

"I'll take one then, but only because I love my son so
dearly. It is my father's heart tells me to take the pound
and be done with it! A strong boy, too, captain. You're
getting a bargain for a pound."

The captain pursed his lips and examined James dubi-
ously again. Finally he shrugged and handed over some
silver to James's father. "Now begone," he said. "We are
ready to cast off."

James started to follow his father, who was hastening
ashore, but Captain Foster seized him and called to a
sailor, "Put him with the others, and hold fast the while.
He has a fancy to leave us."

"Come back!" James screamed at the top of his lungs,
but his father never even turned around. He had got
his pound, and that was to be the end of father and
son. James hated making the admission to himself. He
had always tried to believe that his father really loved
him beneath all the rough treatment. Now he could no
longer carry on the fiction. His father had got rid of
him for a pound, and he hadn't even turned around
for a farewell.

Tears of terror and rejection filled his eyes, and he was so hopeless that he did not resist being led to a hatch with a ladder leading down. He stood there meekly, his eyes still blinded with tears.

"Will you go down yourself, or shall I fling you down?" the sailor demanded. James looked at him wordlessly, only barely seeing him. The sailor seemed to understand some of his shock and bewilderment, because his voice was not so harsh this time when he said, "Go below, boy. No harm will come to you."

Chapter 2

Life at Sea

James obediently started down the ladder, asking himself hopelessly, am I to be a cabin boy? Is that what I am doing here? But if that is it, why am I not put to work at once?

All this time James kept going down, down, with the light growing dimmer at each step. A new smell, of many sweating bodies, rose up to greet him.

His foot found the end of the ladder, and in the blackness he reached the planking of the hold. He stood stiff and still, trying to believe the sailor who had promised him no harm. All around him were the sounds of human voices talking low, of the movements of many bodies. The next few moments were made more confusing by the sound and motion of casting off and the rock of the ship as she made for sea.

"Here, little boy, sit down," a companionable voice reached him. "A little fellow like you, what are they about? Taking a small chap like you!"

James felt his way cautiously toward the owner of the voice, letting his tears fall freely because it was dark. Nobody could see that he wept like a baby. He had to feel his way around people who sat on the floor, following the sound of the friendly voice. When it said reassuringly, "Good, you have found me," he too sat down.

"Come, little boy, tell me what you do here. Is your mother aboard?"

"Oh, sir, my mother has been dead these many years," James said, and gave an inadvertent sob. "I'm twelve, sir," he quavered on.

"Twelve, are you? In fact?"

"Oh, yes, sir, I wouldn't lie, sir."

The other laughed, a very youthful laugh. "I'm only thirteen myself," he said, "so you don't need to 'sir' me. I took you for nine or ten, standing in the bad light on the ladder. You are a bit undersized, though, aren't you?"

James took no offense. The voice was kind.

"So we're almost of an age," the voice continued. "We must be friends, then. You and I are the only lads. There are maids aplenty, and men and women enough. But only you and I for boys."

He asked James his name and James told him, adding fearfully, "What is this? Whither are we bound?"

"Don't you know, then?"

"No," said James, and went no further. He was ashamed to admit that his father had sold him aboard.

"Why, lad, we're bound for America," said his new friend, seeming too eager to talk about the voyage to question James's remarkable ignorance. "We're all going to the new land as bonded servants, every one of us. Me — I'm Davy Butcher — and you, too."

Here was terror upon terror to James. He had heard from one or another of his father's intimate friends that American masters were cruel to their bondsmen past believing, and he wept again, sobbing unashamedly. "We are to be white slaves!"

"Come, now," Davy coaxed. "It's a brave new life we're going to."

"They'll beat us and starve us," James sobbed, dipping into his past for a picture of the future. "Or the Indians will kill us!"

"Indeed they won't," Davy said confidently. "We'll do our job of work to suit our masters, and no man can ask for more. And as for Indians — that's all in the past now."

James was struck dumb with fear at the picture he had made for himself, and Davy's reassurance was no help. His father, without ever having gone to church himself, had always had a great deal to say about religious matters. Memories of his description of the grim Puritans who, he said, had gone to make up the population of America, sent cold shivers through James.

"We will be sitting in church all day," he faltered,

and held his breath until Davy gave his kind, reassuring laugh.

"Oh, to be sure not!" Davy said. "There must be reason in all things. If the Puritans are to get their living, then they cannot in common sense spend more time in church than they can spare from farm or shop or countinghouse. Consider, James, how would they earn their keep?"

James considered and admitted with a somewhat lighter heart that Davy seemed to see things in a more sensible way.

"And besides," Davy went on, "all are not Puritans. That is only in New England, a place of harsh winters and cruel hot summers. There are Catholics in a place called Maryland, and Quakers here and there, and some Jews, too. My uncle made inquiries of the squire, you may be sure, before he engaged to let me set foot aboard the *Eleanora May*. Our squire was the first to admit he had only a faint knowledge of the new land, but he did tell of Catholics and Quakers and Jews."

James could not say what there was in all this to comfort him, but comforted he was and better able to share the cheer in the joys Davy saw waiting for them in the new land. When Davy talked on of paupers who had gone to the colonies, worked their time, and come home wealthy merchants, James began to feel something almost like hope.

"But what is meant by working our time?" James asked. "What time?"

"Aye, there's the rub," Davy said. "We can't escape that! The men and women aboard will be signed to work from three to five years, and then be set free to make their own lives."

"But you and I?" James asked.

"For us it will be a master till we are twenty-one," Davy said. "For me eight years, and for you nine."

"Then God help us," James said.

"There is no cause for tears," Davy said with his wonderful confidence. "Always remember those indentured servants who end up with great farms of their own, or ships, or other wealth."

Once more James was comforted. He did not believe all Davy said, but he loved him for saying it. After a while he ventured shyly, "I hope we get the same master, Davy."

"Indeed, and I hope so too," Davy said. "Then I shall care for you and see to it that you are kindly treated."

"I believe I would like a farmer for a master," James said, growing bold in his wishes.

"Let him be a good teacher, whoever he is," Davy said. "For he must teach us the way we are to make our living the rest of our lives."

A sailor now called down to tell them they might come on deck.

"Aye, it's safe for captain now," a man called out in the darkness. "We're too far from land to leave him, be we ever so good at swimming."

There was a general laugh at this and a stir as the

elders debated among themselves. It was bitter cold, they reminded one another. Still they decided to go above if only for a breath of fresh air. Once out in the sunshine, James had barely time to notice that Davy was a tall, well-grown boy with curly brown hair before he observed something that humiliated him and cast him down. He was the only one dressed in such rags. A moment passed while he stood with his eyes searching the deck, as if by not looking at the others he could prevent them from seeing him. It was only a moment, and then the captain roared to him, "You, boy! Come here."

He ran obediently to the captain, who said, "You'll die on me, dressed that way. Perish of the cold, you will. Come with me."

They went below to another part of the ship, a finer part, the passages lit with lanterns. In one of the cabins the captain opened a chest and searched out a jacket of the type the sailors wore.

"A pound I paid for you, and near half a pound for this coat. With your keep you'll run me a couple of pounds more. I'll never get it back. The trouble is, you have not yet started to get your growth, and so you will look too small to sell."

James could not explain away his size, so he stood humbly until the captain handed him the jacket. He hastened to put it on. The captain said with a laugh, "Now we'll have to send out a search party to find you. But it must do, it's the smallest I have."

The sleeves hung well below his fingers, and the

coat skirt, which was designed to be waist length on a
man, came almost to his knees. It will warm the more of
me, thought James, not unhappy at the idea. He did not
have the courage to say it aloud, and stood politely silent while the captain upbraided him once again for
being so small.

"Never mind," Captain Foster said finally. "You'd be
larger if you could, I suppose."

To this James could honestly answer, "Yes, sir,"
whereupon Captain Foster said, "Get on deck with the
others then."

James obeyed with alacrity. He was proud of his new
jacket and wanted to show it off to Davy. His friend

admired it properly, fingering the wool like a true judge of fabric. "Excellent, to be sure. Does he mean to let you keep it?"

"Indeed, yes," James said gleefully. "He talked of getting the cost back in America."

"Oh, then," said Davy sagely, "you are in our class exactly. He outfitted us all, that we may stay well and look well and so fetch a fair price. He figures me to be worth fifteen pounds."

"You'll fetch more," said James loyally, sighing as he measured his meager worth against Davy's.

For their first meal on board they were fed on a kind of hard biscuit and soup. There was much grumbling at the fare. James, however, found no fault with it. It was far better than he was used to. The soup was tasty, and he welcomed the courage it poured through his body. Davy, too, did not complain.

"Captain Foster is known to run a fair ship," he whispered to James, so the grumblers would not hear. "My uncle learned all he could before he gave me up. My uncle is a good, kind man, only with too many children of his own to keep me now that I'm grown. He would not send me off on any but a good ship, with a decent captain. You'll see, there'll be no plague aboard the *Eleanora May.*"

James was more than satisfied. He was to be warm and fed, and Davy promised him there were no more Indians left in America. He had a friend for the first time in his life and had none of his father's blows and threats

to fear ever again. If it were not for the unknown, waiting for him in the new land, he could have been positively happy.

It seemed at first that the prow of the ship parted
the waves for an even ride, but when the sun sank low
on the horizon, the ship began an ominous roll. James
could hardly keep his footing.

"Are we going to sink?" he cried, terrified.

"No, no," Davy said. "It is only the waves. I have
heard of it. And oh, I have heard of this, too!" He flung
himself against the rail. "Don't be frightened, James," he
said with a groan. "I am only seasick."

Within an hour most of the bondsmen and all the wom-
en had joined Davy in his misery. James felt no twinge
of seasickness himself. He stayed loyally by Davy, finding a way to wet Davy's handkerchief (for he had none
of his own) and use it to wipe his face. He got him the
dry biscuits that the crew said were safest for the seasick to eat. This continued for a full three days and
three nights. Not once during that time did James ever
sit down to eat with more than a handful of his fellow
servants; the rest had lost all interest in food. But finally
the misery passed, the sea grew a little calmer, and the
people more accustomed to the ship's motion. Davy had
strength to smile wryly and say, "And I was going to
care for you!"

"We will care for one another," said James, and Davy
agreed that that was a capital idea.

They had fair winds at their backs now, and the ship

cut a clean path through the water, all sails full. As each
day passed James and Davy talked of their new life,
and James was surer than ever that he would find a
kind master.

The men and women talked too, but their talk was of
a different kind, with less wonder of the future and a
something like arrogance in many of them. From them
the boys learned that the ship was not sailing to Philadelphia, which was the port that saw most indentured
servants. Rather it was headed for a place called Boston. To James this meant little at first, but Davy ex-
pressed real disappointment.

"I was set on Philadelphia," he confessed; then with
a return to his usual high spirits, "But why not Boston,
after all?"

"Why not?" one of the men asked, laughing. "It is
only the largest city in the colonies."

"Nay, second largest. Philadelphia is first," cried another, and the two men went at it, quoting friends and
returned sailors and talk they had heard.

Davy declared himself content. "I did not know Boston was a large city," he admitted. "That is all I ask, a
large city so we will surely find masters who will help
us make our fortunes."

Suddenly James realized what he had at first over-
looked.

"But that is Puritan country," he cried, his voice trem-
bling, and in spite of everything Davy had said, he
saw himself in church forever.

"Aye, and good Christians we'll end up, to be sure,"
Davy said, laughing. "Willy-nilly, we'll say our prayers
and learn our hymns."

Try as he might, James could not join his friend in
laughter at the dreary future he foresaw, nor would Davy
frown over it. "Other men live so and thrive. We will too,"
said Davy, and urged James to listen to how fearless
were the others on board.

Nearly all the men had trades. Of the forty-two men
there were only a few who could not boast of being a
weaver or a joiner or a chandler or a cooper or a miller
or a tailor, and there were a goldsmith and a physician
on board too. There had been a deal of amusement during the seasickness because Dr. Waite, far from being
able to help the others, had been laid low along with
them.

"A fine doctor he is," the people grumbled. But one
among them knew of Dr. Waite by reputation. He told
them that the doctor was indeed a famous physician
and bonesetter. "He's a pet of royalty," he added. Dr.
Waite had set a broken leg for a young duke so perfectly that, once mended, there was no sign of a limp.

"Then why does he run off to hide in the wilderness?"
Davy demanded.

"That I know too. He is a man of extravagant tastes
and is so deep in debt that even his noble friends can't
rescue him. It was either debtor's prison or this, and he
chose this."

Dr. Waite himself did not deign to mingle with the

rest. He had a cabin of his own and ate with the captain. He was said to have a house and servant waiting for him in Boston, arranged for by the very duke whose son he had healed so skillfully.

The rest were all alike in not knowing what the future held for them. The maids and women all claimed they could cook or called themselves seamstresses or spinsters or dairy maids. One was a milliner who carried herself with an air and fancied herself too fine for the rest.

"They will all be snatched up," Davy predicted. "You will see when we get to Boston. When a boatload of servants come in, the people come to the wharves or come on deck to find what they need. They pick us out as if we were goods on a shop shelf."

James did not much like this picture of what would happen, but with Davy at his side his courage stayed high and his hopes remained steady.

you're keeping him for yourself. And what's this?" He
poked a sharp finger into James's middle. "Babes, is it?
I'll not have him."

"He's a full twelve, and strong, Beaton, though it may
not appear so at first sight," said Captain Foster. Beaton
laughed unpleasantly, but the captain went on calmly,
"You know how it is with small people, all their strength
is husbanded and not wasted in growing."

James wondered at this view of it, for he knew that
from the time of giving him his jacket Captain Foster had
not once taken heed of him. But now the captain talked
very knowledgeably of James, and of how he was willing and courteous, and all but brimming over with
strength. It seemed clear to James, through his panic at
being sold to the brute named Beaton, that the captain's
glib tongue must win. Captain Foster repeated that he
had promised his friend a boy and had always meant
Davy to be that boy. There was no use talking, he said.
The boy Davy must go to his friend.

Beaton spat on the deck and said, "I'll have the boy
Davy, or I'll have none of them."

He half turned, as if to go, and now the captain
seemed to be torn between avarice and friendship. He
wanted to give his friend the better boy, yet he didn't
want to be out of pocket by it. James thought the captain
might still have his way, for he seemed to be a famous
bargainer. He was sure of it when the captain said craft-
ily, "You may have the little one for half what you pay
for the others."

"Have him? I wouldn't have him for nothing — not even if you gave me something to boot. He's a liability. Come to terms, Foster! If you don't hasten, I'll have to feed and shelter them overnight, and it all costs, you know, cuts into the profits."

They haggled for a while, the buyer insisting on Davy, the captain steadily refusing. "But I promised my friend Waldruss a boy," he said repeatedly, "how can I disappoint him?"

Finally Beaton said disgustedly, "Very well, if you can afford to be ten pounds out of pocket, keep him. Keep them both. Keep them all."

"All right, then," the captain said hastily. "Take him. Waldruss is a good sort, he'll make do with the little one."

In minutes the money changed hands, ten pounds each for the men and for Davy as well. When the buyer grumbled over paying ten pounds for a boy, Captain Foster said sarcastically, "Ah, yes, you are being cheated! Before the hour is out you'll have retailed them for a profit of five pounds a head." He paused, looked out onto the water of the harbor, and said in an undertone, "Go, then! Here is my friend Waldruss, and I won't have him see that fine lad. Be off!"

Beaton had handed a stout rope over to a sailor, who made the men and Davy fast to one another in a series of links. He now tied an end of the rope to his own wrist, and led them off.

"Good-bye, Davy!" James called, and because they

might never meet again, and there went his only friend, he burst into tears. Davy looked as if he would like to cry too, but he held his head high. As if incapable of speech, he waved a hand in farewell. They looked like a train of animals following one another. James watched them out of sight.

"Why are you so small?" Captain Foster asked the familiar question. "Dry your eyes the while, or I'll have no hope of convincing Waldruss you're even twelve."

James had no heart to answer. In any event the captain had moved away and now stood at the side, shouting, "Ahoy, the *Annie B.*!"

A rope ladder was let down to a small sailing vessel that carried two men. One of these clambered aboard. This was Mr. Waldruss, for Captain Foster called him by name and greeted him with every sign of friendship.

"My Cousin Beadle was sailing his shallop into Boston, and so I came along on the chance the *Eleanora May* had docked. And so here you are, Foster."

James watched and listened with a fast-beating heart, cautiously seeming to stare out to sea but almost wild to learn what manner of man Mr. Waldruss might be.

In appearance Mr. Waldruss was hale and strong. He wore neither hat nor wig, and his brown hair hung to his shoulders. He wore a leather jerkin, but it was open, as if in his strength he needed no defense against the brisk winter wind. But his clothes, his full brown shirt and breeches, put in James's mind the clear thought that a man who dressed so soberly could be nothing but a Puritan! And yet he was not, in himself, a frightening man. Aside from being very tall and very broad, a large man altogether, James could not tell anything about him. He could not decide whether a boy would find kindness in him — or not.

Chapter 4

James Has A Master

"And who's this lad?" Mr. Waldruss asked suddenly. James's blood seemed to stand still, caught between hope and fear.

"Why, here's the boy you told me to look out for you," said the captain. He spoke with such jovial enthusiasm that James found it hard to believe he had only just finished trying to get rid of him. "As fine a worker as any youth in the land, for all his size. A bit young perhaps at only twelve, but time will take care of that."

Mr. Waldruss looked very thoughtfully at James. "Yes, his face shows him to be twelve, and more. A face full of troubles. He's undersized." He shook his head. "I was to ask you if you had a boy for my neighbor — have you no others?"

"None," said Captain Foster. "Your neighbor is in bad luck, and you are in good. Snatch him up while you can."

Again Captain Foster made his speech about James's surprising strength, but Mr. Waldruss seemed scarcely to listen. Suddenly he said, "Come here, boy, and tell me your name."

James moved closer in slow, timid steps and answered.

"Well, James, and are you a good boy?"

"Yes, sir," James barely whispered.

"And will you be willing to rise before dawn and work a farmer's hard day, eh?"

A farmer! Tears of gratitude filled his eyes. He could not speak, but nodded.

"He's very young," Mr. Waldruss said doubtfully to the captain. "I said a boy of fifteen."

"Boys of fifteen are not so easy to come by honestly," the captain said. "By kidnaping, yes. You've heard of the kidnapers they call 'spiriters' who steal youths off the street? But otherwise a boy is hard to come by honestly. Take him, Waldruss. I'll let you have him cheap. Ten pounds." At the decisive shake of Waldruss' head, "Five, then, since we're old friends."

James listened with fear and wonder and hope as the men arranged between them in what manner the five pounds was to be paid — in so much pork, and so many geese, and so many cheeses, and so many hen's eggs, until everything ran together in his mind.

Then the men shook hands on it, and Waldruss pocketed the paper the captain signed. "Come, boy," he said, and James knew he had a master. And not an unkind one, he told himself with a small beginning of comfort. Mr. Waldruss did indeed seem to be not unkind.

Even as his heart lifted for himself, James had a sad thought for Davy. Poor Davy! His good looks and fine growth had done him a poor service, making him so desirable to the servant peddler. Who knew what kind

of a master he might get now? By a strange trick his
own smallness had done him a favor and secured for
him a master who promised to be a good one.

Mr. Waldruss helped him over the side to the ladder
and so into the shallop. The man who had been waiting
in the small sailboat had something of the look of Mr.
Waldruss, although he was on a smaller scale altogether.
He took a look at James and burst into laughter.

"This is your indentured servant, is it?" he asked.
"This is your plowman and harvester and stableman?"

"Come, Cousin Beadle," Mr. Waldruss said good-na-
turedly. "Welcome James, do not laugh at him. Alone in
a strange land as he is! He's a good boy and will work
with a will. He has time for much growing yet, and he
may not end as he begins. At any rate it is not his fault
he is small."

"Nay, then, it is not," said Mr. Waldruss' cousin, with
good humor. He gave James a friendly pat on the head
that almost knocked him over the side. "And yet I'll be
surprised if with the best will in the world he can lift the
bucket once he's milked the cow."

Mr. Waldruss' cousin was a simple man, who lived by
the ocean and took his living from it. He was a fisherman, and it was with a load of fish that he had come
to Boston today. The fish had been sold and unloaded
before they came for James, but the shallop still stank
of fish and probably always did.

The trip from Boston to Shoreham went quickly, with
a spanking breeze behind them. Cousin Beadle was as in-

quisitive as any old lady gossip. The ride from the harbor to the log jetty before his cottage seemed shortened by his lively interest in every small detail of the transaction that had just passed.

"What paid you for this little James?" he inquired. "Eh, cheap enough, but what you paid for is no great bargain. And had Captain Foster a boy for your neighbor Cotter?"

"No, only James."

"I should have known," said his kin. "Because if you could have got another you would not have taken this one."

"Enough!" said Mr. Waldruss sharply.

"Aye, enough. And I am glad there was no boy for Cotter. How could you have undertaken to get one for him?"

"I did nothing and would have done nothing save tell Cotter if there had been a boy for him. Nothing more. And by the time he could have got to Boston, going overland, any boy would surely have been taken."

"Overland it would have been for Cotter!" said Cousin Beadle forcefully. "My shallop is not for hire to put a servant boy into such hands as that."

There was silence after this, giving James time to shudder with gratitude at his escape from such a master as this Cotter must be.

Mr. Waldruss helped Cousin Beadle tie his shallop to the tiny jetty and politely refused an invitation into the cottage. He pointed to the rising moon.

"I can't find my way without moonlight," he said. "I'd best take it while I can."

The sounds of their arrival brought a young woman, hardly more than a girl, out of the house. This was Cousin Beadle's daughter Annie. She kept house for him, Cousin Beadle being a widower.

"You've come in good time," she said. "A good evening to you, Cousin Waldruss. And so this is your boy?" She came closer and peered at James. "He's full young," she said.

She was a pretty girl, with a brisk and dancing way, but that was not alone what James liked about her. She did not mention his size! He took this as a special favor. He was grateful for small kindnesses, and Annie always remained a favorite of his, from that time on.

"I have a fowl on the spit," she said. "You must all be hungry."

James was all too ready to eat. He waited hopefully for his master's acceptance, but again Mr. Waldruss said they would not stop.

The moon was full up now, but with the loss of the sun the wind from the sea freshened and grew sharp. To James it was like needles in his face. Mr. Waldruss lifted him up easily to sit on the horse before him, and they set out. James began to shiver. He was tired from a sleepless night and a day of uncommonly great nervous strain. He was famished for food, and in spite of the fact that Mr. Waldruss had so far been all he could hope for in a master, he was terrified at the strangeness of everything and the not knowing what lay ahead.

"We could not go home this night were it not for the moon to light our way," Mr. Waldruss said. It was James's first time on a horse and might have been worrisome but that Mr. Waldruss held him so fast. Even so he was far from easy. The meadows seemed endless. The road through the woods was made eerie by the sharp shadows of the leafless boughs and the cries of some night creatures.

When at last they broke clear of the trees to the sight of a candle-glow in a distant window, he was terrified anew. Mr. Waldruss did not frighten him, but there was surely a Mrs. Waldruss, and probably children. How would they receive him?

He stiffened with more than cold the closer they got and welcomed it when Mr. Waldruss delayed their entrance into the house by saying, "We must stable the horse before we go in. This may be your first lesson as a farmer, James. Always look to the beasts first, for they cannot help themselves and their very lives depend on your thought for them."

James slid off the horse, Mr. Waldruss holding him firmly until his feet touched ground. James helped open the heavy doors. From inside came the stampings and calls of the animals disturbed in their rest. Mr. Waldruss called out gently, "Yes, now; there, now," and the sounds grew less.

"If there were not this moon, we would have to fetch light from the house," Mr. Waldruss said, leading the horse into the dimness. He took off saddle and bridle and said, "Mark where I hang them, James, that you will know where each belongs."

James, fearful, dogged Mr. Waldruss as closely as he dared. He watched as his master hung the leather bridle on one peg, the makeshift saddle on another. He was so intent on staying close to his master that he had no idea of what lay behind him. When he turned it was to look into the face of a cow, large to begin with and seeming larger because of the dimness that gave her no limits. He started back with a loud cry of fear, jumping so far he struck Mr. Waldruss amidships.

"Here, here," Mr. Waldruss said, once he had saved himself and James from capsizing. "Afraid of a gentle bossy cow, James?"

"She is so large, sir," James gasped. "I have never seen one so large."

"That I will believe," Mr. Waldruss said, leading James outside and securing the doors again. "My father told me often of the sad little creatures that go for cows in England. Starved and underfed, they were, and not cared for during the long winter. We have a better breed here. Good food and good treatment have made them so."

James trotted rapidly to keep up with Mr. Waldruss. A small spark of hope had started to glow in him. If cows could be made larger by better feeding, might he not have a chance with the same treatment? It seemed he must pray for one more thing, then — good food, and enough of it, to help him to grow.

Chapter 5

James Has A Bath

Now he stood before the house that was to see his servitude. It was all of wood, with two windows showing on this side. James hung back, wishing he could have a hint of the kind of life he was to lead there. Mr. Waldruss lifted the latch, and in an instant they were inside with the heavy door shut behind them.

A bright fire burned in the fireplace, and besides the candle in the window there was one other, on a table made of planks. The rest of the very large room was in shadows. On the side near the fireplace he saw a great bed, but this was all he could be sure of. After a second or two, when his eyes had grown accustomed to the light, he could make out the shape of a woman. He could not really see her, though, not clearly enough to know if she smiled or frowned. She was a slight, short woman, but because he was so afraid of everything in his new life, she was a threat too. He held his breath, waiting.

"Here you are, then, both of you," she called out in a cheery voice. "And both hungry, my word for it."

James breathed out.

"James, is it?" she repeated, when she had been told his name. "A fine name, and a manly one. Sit you down, then."

She came closer with each word, and James could see her face was one made for smiles. This time he took a long breath in, one of relief and hope.

There was a large wooden dish with a loaf of bread on the table. James sat politely, waiting to be told to eat. Instead he had to sit while Mr. Waldruss bent his head and said a prayer. This was the first time James had heard grace, and although the complaints from inside him made him impatient, he bowed his head like his master and sat perfectly still. He listened for the first time to thanks being given for food.

When Mr. Waldruss' prayer was ended, James raised his head cautiously. Observing that his master was now industriously breaking off hunks of the loaf, he raised his head the rest of the way and took a piece as Mr. Waldruss said, "Go ahead, James."

Mrs. Waldruss set before them a pewter pitcher full of milk. James ate ravenously. He had had milk once or twice before and enjoyed it, but now it seemed even more delicious. The bread was firm and tasty. He knew

they were both pleased and amused at his appetite, but
he hardly attended. He ate on industriously while his
master made a more leisurely meal.

"Is all well with the children?" Mr. Waldruss asked
his wife.

"All well, and they were starved for sleep from their
day of mischief. And did you — " she seemed to hesitate
" — did you find a boy for our neighbor Cotter?"

"No," he answered shortly, and she burst out, "I'm so
glad!"

"What do you take me for, woman?" Mr. Waldruss
seemed almost angry. "Did you believe I'd put a boy
into Cotter's hands? The man asked me to find out if
Captain Foster had a boy to sell. I could do no less than
ask. And now I'll tell him there is no boy to be had,"
he concluded with evident satisfaction, "and no harm
done."

"I am much relieved," she said again.

James heard all this, but he had no interest in it because he was beset by a serious worry. The milk pitcher
was empty. He picked it up to pour more milk into his
mug and found not a drop left. He set it down again
carefully and did not look at it again. He must feign.
He did not wish his master to think him a glutton or
that he would eat up more than his service would be
worth. Besides, he had no courage for asking for more.
He was still hungry, but this was no new condition for
him. This would only be one more night he would go to
sleep hungry.

"Have we no more milk?" Mr. Waldruss asked suddenly. Mrs. Waldruss went to a part of the room that was far from the fire. It must be nearly as cold as the outdoors there, James thought. He watched with relief as she refilled the pitcher from a wooden bucket.

James sat unbelieving as she poured milk into his mug. All he could eat, and a kind man for a master, and a good woman for a mistress! No boy could ask for more. James did not believe there was more.

The house seemed to be all one room, but in the shadows there was a ladderlike flight of steps leading up into what must be an attic room. When James could eat and drink no more, he thought he would be told to go up to the attic to sleep, but instead Mrs. Waldruss said, "Now you promised, Eben. You said before he slept — "

"Ah, yes, James," Mr. Waldruss said, laughing a little. "It is a woman's way, my boy. You must have a wash."

James protested. He felt clean, he said. But Mrs. Waldruss already had a wooden tub near the fire, and was pouring hot water into it from one of two large kettles that had been bubbling there. When she had added a little cold water she tested the mixture with her hand and said, "It is just right, I shall turn my back, James," and then he realized for the first time that he was expected to get into the tub naked!

He did not dare argue. At Mr. Waldruss' command he took off his jacket and then, unwillingly, the rags he had never had off his back since first he put them on.

"My wife's good soap will do the trick," Mr. Waldruss said with a chuckle. He lathered James from head to foot. When he had been rinsed off, the water was so dirty that Mr. Waldruss said, "I'm sorry, James, but we must do it again," and emptied the tub outside while James stood dripping by the fire. He refilled the tub from the second kettle, and lathered James again.

At last James was clean enough to suit his master. He dressed in a pair of Mr. Waldruss' breeches. The legs had to be rolled up many times, and the waist tied tight with a strip of old linen. The shirt he put on, from the same source, hung to his heels. None of it mattered. He gave a giant yawn. The bath had finished what the warmth and the meal had started. He was so sleepy he could barely keep his eyes open. He stood, swaying a little, while Mrs. Waldruss said, "Stand away from the door that you don't catch a chill, but open it again I must. I won't have these clothes in my house overnight. Tomorrow I'll wash them and — mercy on us, the boy's a towhead!"

Mr. Waldruss gave a surprised laugh and said, "So he is. Until now we could not tell for the grime. A right handsome little lad you are, James, and I don't doubt a good one. We shall get along famously."

He gave James a lighted candle and said, "Blow it out as soon as you see your way abovestairs, James. A fire is all too easy to set. Besides there is no sense in wasting candles. Waste not, want not. I have made you a room of your own, away from the little ones. As soon as you are in it, you must put out your light."

James climbed up, holding the candle above his head. He shivered a little more with each step. In the attic itself the chill seemed to spring at him. He held the candle high and looked about him. A small room had been made by putting a wall across a corner of the attic. An opening had been left as a doorway.

In the large space that was left, a big bed held several
children asleep. James went quickly through the door to
his room and saw a pallet made up for him on the floor.
He blew out his candle, took off his shoes, and huddled
under the quilt that he was to learn was feather-filled.
He did not expect to be able to sleep in such cold, but
in a surprisingly short time a wonderful warmth began
to comfort him, and he drifted off.

Chapter 6

Davy Is Found

It was still dark when a childish voice said softly in his ear, "My father wants you."

James scrambled off the pallet and into his boots, then went clattering down the steps.

"Sir," he gasped, "you wanted me?"

"Don't be frightened, lad," Mr. Waldruss said. "It's near dawn. We must see to the beasts."

Telling me not to be frightened is like whistling into the wind, James thought, ashamed. I am afraid of all and of everything. But he calmed down at Mr. Waldruss' words and looked at the girl who had called him. She was now coming down the ladder at a more sedate rate. She was a girl of about ten, who hung shyly about her mother.

"Come, Elizabeth, welcome James," her father said. "She is our great girl, is Elizabeth, our eldest girl of four."

But Elizabeth hung her head and looked away, behavior that James welcomed since he did not know what he would answer if she spoke to him.

Mrs. Waldruss said, "There will be cornmeal mush for you when you get back. You'll like that, won't you?"

James was sure he would, although he had no idea what it was. He was hungry again, quite as if he had not eaten so much at bedtime. He would in fact have been more satisfied to sit down and eat right now, before he did any work, but he dutifully and unprotestingly followed his master to the barn.

"I expect very little of you at first, so try not to be so fearful," Mr. Waldruss said.

James gulped, "Thank you, sir," but he could not make himself be easy. He was used to a different sort of man, and he expected Mr. Waldruss to turn into that sort at any minute. He would not have been surprised at a shower of blows — he was only surprised at its absence.

He watched in the candlelight — for it was barely dawn — as his master showed him how the stalls were swept out. "This we do not do every day during the winter, although with you to help me it will be more often," Mr. Waldruss said. With his birch broom he pushed the sweepings out of the barn into a pile covered by snow. "This will all find good use in the spring to mix with the earth and help us to a good crop."

James listened earnestly as Mr. Waldruss explained and instructed, but mainly he thought of the meal waiting for him. He dreaded, even in the warm, clean clothes he now wore, the freezing walk back to the house from the barn. Yet when Mr. Waldruss said they would go back, he almost bounded ahead in his eagerness. He restrained himself just in time. He must never forget he was a servant boy with a master to please.

Three more little girls had now joined their sister Elizabeth. James stood awkwardly, interested in nothing so much as food, and uncertain of his welcome from the girls. The child who seemed next in age to Elizabeth came forward suddenly and said gaily, "You are James! And you and I shall be trenchermates!"

"Indeed not, Hitty!" Elizabeth said, clearly displeased. "You and I are trenchermates, as older sisters should be, and shall remain so. Besides," she added, "as you well know, Hitty, James is to have a trencher to himself."

James, who had never had a dish of his own, waited with awe as his flat wooden plate was placed into his hands. Benches were arranged about the table, and James, watching the others, lined up behind them as they went to the fireplace for Mrs. Waldruss to ladle mush from the pot.

He now learned that Mrs. Waldruss was a great talker on little things. She kept up a stream of unimportant chatter: "Hitty, love, do be still. You jump about like a hare," or, "Rachel, mind your sister behind you and do

not step backwards," and to the baby, a child who barely toddled about, "Mary, there's a love, you are trying
to be a great girl, but Rachel will carry the trencher
for you both."

Since Elizabeth and Hitty shared a trencher, only Elizabeth was needed to carry it; and Hitty was thus free
to fetch milk and bread and set about wooden spoons.
James now observed that all the tableware except the
mugs was of wood.

"Now that you have come, James, we have used our
last mug but one," Hitty volunteered. "If we have a
guest, we must empty the money mug to serve him."

Her eyes went to the one remaining mug that stood
on the mantel over the fireplace.

"Empty the money mug," Mr. Waldruss said with a
laugh. "That's an easy job, that! There's little enough
in it."

The trenchers had been sliced from the round of a
tree and had been slightly scooped out. They were fash-
ioned by hand, and Mr. Waldruss, seeing James stare,
said he had made them himself.

"There's more to eat, James," Mrs. Waldruss said as she
spooned the yellow stuff onto his trencher. "I give you
this small amount to taste."

James looked shyly up to her and then into the pot.
There was indeed plenty. He sat at the table but did not
start to eat no matter how he wished to, because he
saw that nobody else took a bite. He remembered yes-

terday's grace. All waited for Mrs. Waldruss to join them
and then for Mr. Waldruss' prayer.

When at last he could eat, he found the mush entirely
to his taste. He polished off his first helping in jig time.
There was fried ham to go with it. He had more — and
more — and more. It was as if he had twelve years of
emptiness to fill at each meal.

After they had helped their mother tidy the room,
Elizabeth and Hitty were told to take James with them
when they went to the henyard.

"Show him about the farm," their father said, and Mrs.
Waldruss chattered along, "Do, girls, and mind you don't
go into the woods and lose yourselves."

James thought this a pointless warning, since the
woods were a good half-mile off. He saw that even the
well-behaved girls did not attend. He was to learn that
Mrs. Waldruss, though a good-hearted woman, seemed
to live by alarms and fears of things that never happened, with a spicing of her insatiable interest in every
concern of everyone she knew.

James did not overmuch like leaving the warmth indoors, although he would not dream of refusing. But
the cold was so bitter that the girls did not like it either,
and having gathered the eggs they returned, complain-
ing of the weather.

"James and I will go out together, then," their father
said. "As soon as he is warm again. I fear more snow.
We must bring in enough wood to see us through."

When a little time had passed James confessed that he was warm again, honest in spite of his wishes. This time Mr. Waldruss wrapped a wool scarf firmly over James's ears, doing it himself with a gentleness surprising in those great hands. Instantly the cold seemed halved. James was beginning to learn that kindness from one to another made life easier.

Mr. Waldruss had cut up a maple he had felled in his own field. They carried logs of all sizes into the house, stacking them against the walls on either side of the fireplace. Some were so large James could not even move them, and these Mr. Waldruss handled, swinging them about as if they were kindling.

When they had filled all the space they could, and after they had come inside to stay and seated themselves by the fireplace, Mr. Waldruss said, "There is little real work for us in the winter, James. It will be a good two months before we plow. Till then I plan to send you to school."

"School, sir?" James repeated blankly. "I wish only to be a farmer."

"And a farmer you'll be," Mr. Waldruss said. "A good one, I hope — and all the better for someday being able to sign your own name to your own deed."

James sat in silence, thinking of the great things that had happened to him in the short time since he had been in the new land. Goodness surrounded him. The kindness of his master, all the food he could eat, and now — school!

As he sat musing, Mr. Waldruss pointed to a great slab of wood that had been much cut out and gouged, and said, "I mean to hew me an ox-yoke this winter from yon solid block, James. This will be my work while you are at school. I have worked on it all winter at odd times. It will be ready for the plowing."

"Halloo, Waldruss," a loud voice boomed from outside. Mr. and Mrs. Waldruss gave a quick, guarded look at one another, and Mr. Waldruss went to the door and opened it.

"Come in, Cotter," Mr. Waldruss said. A short, broad-shouldered man entered, slapping his arms against his chest. James thought him ugly. His full lips seemed set in a sneer, as if they knew no other way of behaving.

"I'm on my way home — came overland from Boston and slept the night at my brother's."

James realized from hearing this what a saving in time the sea route from Boston was.

"I was going to ride over to tell you I have no news of a boy for you," Mr. Waldruss said, but Mr. Cotter laughed heavily and said, "I found one for myself. A fine strong boy. What's this?" he asked, catching sight of James.

"The boy Captain Foster brought me," Mr. Waldruss said.

Mr. Cotter stared. "You paid for *him*?"

"James is a good boy," Mr. Waldruss said sharply, sending a warm feeling of gratitude through James. "Come closer to the fire, Cotter. It is bitter cold out there."

"Aye, that's why I broke my journey here, to warm myself for the mile left to me."

"So you found a boy, did you?" Mr. Waldruss asked, while Mrs. Waldruss, strangely silent, poured a mug of ale for Mr. Cotter.

"Happened on him in Boston," Mr. Cotter said boastfully. "A man was leading a string of men and this boy, all with indentures to sell. Fifteen pounds I paid, and a bargain."

Before he had half finished, almost as soon as he had begun, James knew that the boy Mr. Cotter had bought was Davy Butcher! He went very close to Mr. Waldruss and said in a whisper, "I believe it is my friend. Would you ask him, sir?"

Mr. Waldruss asked and was told that his new servant was indeed named Davy and that he was at this minute outside exercising his master's horse against the cold.

Without stopping for permission James flew out into the bleak day and ran to the tall form stalking valiantly against the cold. It took only half a look for Davy to take in the situation. The two boys hugged one another. James was close to heaven. Davy, his strong friend Davy, was to be only a mile away! It was a moment for joy — and thoughtlessness.

"Come inside and be warm," James invited heedlessly, forgetting he and Davy were both indentured servants, bound to masters until their twenty-first birthday, and with no rights to issue or to accept invitations.

They stabled Mr. Cotter's horse and went unquestion-

Chapter 7

James Goes to School

Simon Cotter was a tall, well-grown boy of fifteen. He came to the door well after sunup, while James sat finishing his breakfast. James had expected Davy to come with Simon and innocently asked for his friend.

"That scum?" Simon retorted when James made his shy inquiry. "What does he want with book learning?"

"The same thing James does and you do," Mrs. Waldruss said in her sprightly way. "I suppose your father needed his help about the house and could not spare him today. Tomorrow will do as well."

But whatever Mrs. Waldruss believed, James was sure Davy would never be sent to school. He judged by listening to how Simon talked. In this case as in many others to come in the future, he proved himself wiser than his mistress. She, without being foolish or silly, would frequently see a fancy as a fact. She had a tendency to presume that the results she wished for would follow in spite of all the opposite hints and promises along the way.

James made ready to go. His spirits were somewhat shaken by his disappointment at not seeing Davy and beginning to be depressed the more because of the newness that lay ahead. Matters were not helped by the mean nature of his companion. Indeed Simon seemed to have come prepared to snicker at James, because a first look was all he needed to say, with an air of great astonishment, "How small you are. Are you indeed twelve?"

But here a strange thing happened. James was not crushed by this sneer! The truth was, James was being armored each minute of every hour to withstand this kind of treatment. There was a feeling of kindness and love all through the Waldruss house. His master seemed to feel some people were small, and some large, and left it at that.

Mrs. Waldruss, on the other hand, frequently said, "Eat more, do, James. You must make up for years gone by."

By the calm acceptance of his size by the one, and the determination to change it by the other, James was encouraged to accept himself as he was and yet to hope for improvement.

Just before Simon arrived and as James ate the generous portions Mrs. Waldruss put before him, he asked her, "Do you really believe, ma'am, that it is not too late for me to eat myself into a larger size?"

"Why, bless me," she said, "you have not begun to grow! Time and good food may accomplish great things for you, James boy. I mind me a cousin — Japeth, his name is — Japeth Skinner — no, that is my cousin that was left overnight in the snow as a babe, and no harm come to him that could ever be found out. It was my cousin Jacob I meant. Jacob Turner. His mother had been a Plankett, and they were all small people, though very honest, my word for it. And poor Jacob could not accept his smallness as the will of God, and always stamped his little foot and screamed in a most unfortunate way whenever his smallness was mentioned."

She stopped and busied herself about the fireplace, and it soon became clear that she felt she had finished her tale. James prodded her diffidently. "And did he remain small forever, ma'am?"

"Did I not tell you?" she asked, amazed. "He grew into a large man who had to deny himself food for fear of being too tall to enter a door and too wide besides."

"How did it happen, then?" James asked eagerly, prepared instantly to do whatever Cousin Jacob had done to accomplish the same end.

"Oh, it simply came to pass, as time went by. We never gave over remarking on it, and neither I am sure would you, if you had been there. It was a truly wonderful thing. You will see, one day."

Her tales all ended this way, in a sort of promise that great things lay in store for him.

Thus on this first day of school, James did not reply to Simon's jibes. He got his jacket, fresh and clean now that Mrs. Waldruss had finished with it, and went off, still a little fearful, but only at the newness of it all. He was surprised at himself for not minding Simon more but decided it must be that having had nothing, less than nothing, all his life, to find himself part of a family dedicated to affection and industry could protect him from most of the small teasing pains of the world.

School was kept in the house of the minister, a young, earnest man named Stedman.

"He must eke out a living this way," Simon said, as full of spite against the minister as he had been against James or Davy. He seemed to take an immense pleasure in reporting anything of disadvantage to another. "Our minister Stedman is promised fifty pounds a year and gets none of it in money. It is all cordwood and corn and homespuns and stock. But he must have some cash, and so he keeps a school."

When Mr. Stedman learned that James could neither read nor write, he said kindly, "We'll soon mend that," and gave him all his attention at first.

Until now James had feared what church might hold for him on the Sunday. Mr. Waldruss had told him they would all attend, but now he felt more comfortable about it. Mr. Stedman was friendly and almost gentle

— but he was to learn that Mr. Stedman the teacher and Mr. Stedman the minister were as much like two different people as one man could be.

To James it was a great wonder that he should be sitting in a school. He began to learn his letters just like the great lords in the old country. Without being eager about his education, for it was a new idea to him and would take getting used to, he was still anxious to please Mr. Waldruss. He applied himself with a whole heart.

When he went home that afternoon, he had still another defense against Simon Cotter — the words of Mr. Stedman, spoken as he left: "Well done, James Porter!"

He reported on his day to the Waldruss family and

was met with encouragement on all sides. Mrs. Waldruss watched proudly as he picked out the letters he had learned, and Hitty declared, "I have learned all my letters and will help you."

The girls did not go to school. Whatever education they could scramble into at home might be theirs, but it seemed they were not to be sent to school. This did not surprise James in the least. Girls did not need education to keep house and spin.

As usual he was famished. Tomorrow would be baking day, and the only bread left was a stale flat-tasting thing called pumpkin bread. Mrs. Waldruss presented it apologetically. "We must stretch our cornmeal, you know, and so mix it with pumpkin."

James found no fault with it. The idea that he could eat until he was full was what he found hardest to believe! But nobody stopped him. Indeed, twice Elizabeth brought more of the bread and for him alone. The others spurned it, eating only what they must of it.

Before many days more had passed, Mrs. Waldruss had knitted him a pair of mittens from the yarn of an old muffler and altered an old shirt of Mr. Waldruss' to fit him. In time James went off each morning dressed as warm as any child with a mother to love him.

The Waldrusses were regular in their attendance at church. James, on his first Sunday, after listening to Mr. Stedman's sermon on true piety, came away with the troubled sensation that neither he nor the Waldrusses had any sure hope of salvation.

True, they had sat and shivered without footwarmers
or any heat save the pieces of woolen homespun they
wrapped about their feet. Mr. Stedman did not approve
of footwarmers, and the congregation being all farmers
and fisherfolk, he had nothing to complain of there, for
they could not afford to buy any. Again, they had all
walked to church. Mr. Stedman did not approve of riding on the Sabbath, and the Waldrusses could not have
done it in any event, the trail through the woods being
wide enough only for a horse, not for a cart. There
being only one horse, they had no choice.

James had the impression that Mr. Waldruss would
have dared Mr. Stedman's wrath if he had either a suf-
ficiency of horses or a wider road. His master did not
seem sobered or scared by Mr. Stedman's sermon.

Once out of church, in fact, Mr. Waldruss hoisted Rachel to his shoulders as playfully as if it were an ordinary weekday, and James, after a timid moment, followed suit with little Mary. It was only kind — the tots
were wearied by the long walk and the longer stay in
church.

"Why so serious, James?" Mr. Waldruss asked suddenly. "Is Mr. Stedman's sermon not to your liking? I
thought you sat very straight and still throughout and
must commend you on it."

"I was proud of you, my word for it," Mrs. Waldruss
echoed. "None of the fidgeting about and squirming of
some little girls."

Elizabeth and Hitty giggled, and James stiffened. Mr.

Stedman had especially warned against youthful levity on the Sabbath.

"I suppose," Mr. Waldruss went on, "that after church in the old country, we seem a little stiff and long-winded."

"Sir," James confessed, "I never went to church in England. This is my first time in any church."

Mr. Waldruss looked sharply at him. "So this was your first time," he said thoughtfully. "And you had to sit through an hour of prayer and an hour of Stedman's sermon, and you are thinking of your sins, eh?"

"Yes, sir," James said in a whisper.

Mr. Waldruss seemed to consider before he spoke again.

"My father was a Puritan, James. He came during the troubles with the second Charles. I suppose if you must put a name to me, Puritan it would be. But James, don't let Stedman's sermon frighten you. He must demand all, in the hope of getting half. You are a good boy and do your work as well as you can. I believe the Lord smiles on such. What value would you be in His eyes if you shirked during the week only to spend all of the Sabbath in His praise?"

This put a new view on it, but still James was worried. He shook his head a little. "Mr. Stedman said that we must beware of vanity, and I am vain of my new clothes: and that we must be grave all day today, and I am wanting to run and jump because I grew stiff with sitting. And he said we must think of things of the spirit, and yet as I speak I am thinking of Mrs. Waldruss' good cooking and the meal we will sit down to."

"Aye, aye," Mr. Waldruss said with a smile. "You list sin after sin. I will tell you what you must do, James. Do you go on as you were, working and eating with a will, and be as grave as a lad your age can be on the Sabbath. I will watch carefully. When I feel you are sinning in the eyes of God I will bring you up sharp."

"Oh, will you, sir, indeed?" James asked, with immense relief.

"Do not fear. I am a hard man on a sinner," Mr. Waldruss assured him with such a sign of laughter in his voice that James felt completely unburdened of his fears. Little Mary on his shoulders seemed all at once feather-light, and he went the rest of the way home humming a tune, though it was the Sabbath.

Chapter 8

Springtime Plans

In the schooling that lay before him until spring, James learned not only to read a little and to sign his name but to do simple ciphering besides. The running of the sap in the sugar trees, the maples, was the signal of school's end for him.

There was still snow on the ground, so Mr. Waldruss and James went into the woods riding on something called a *pung*. This Indian name described a wagonlike, wooden box fixed on sleigh runners, with shafts for a horse. Into the wagon part they put deep troughs and buckets made of wood. Iron being so costly and hard to come by, the buckets were bound with wood too. Mr. Waldruss told James he had bartered sheep's wool with a Boston cooper for the buckets.

They brought with them an iron boiling kettle, axes, and provisions. Mr. Waldruss carried a firearm with ammunition, in case of wolves or bear.

The Cotters met them at the site — Mr. Cotter, Simon, their black boy Catto, and Davy.

The men "boxed" the trees. James watched, fascinated, as they went about getting the sap in the Indian manner, cutting a deep slanting gash into the wood and scooping it out so that the sap gathered in the cut and from there dripped into a wooden trough set below. Two of the sugar trees had died standing, and the men agreed that it was from the previous year's boxing. The trees had been scooped out too deeply.

"We must be more cautious in future," Mr. Waldruss declared.

James and Davy had little time for talk, with the jealous eyes of Simon on them constantly, but James noted with sorrow that his friend was thinner and that his merry smile was mostly absent.

"He's a hard man," Davy whispered in answer to James's question. James could not doubt it, from the way the Cotters both snapped and snarled at Davy and Catto.

When the sun was high, the men called to Catto and the boys that they would eat. James and Davy sat together, and although they could not stop Simon and Catto from joining them, there was a satisfaction in being side by side. All four sat on a felled tree as they ate, while the two masters sat on the pung, a little aside, and discussed and planned the day's business.

The two servant boys ate hastily by a whispered agreement. Then James, feeling safer with his master, asked boldly, "Sir, may Davy and I explore until you are finished?"

"I can only answer yes for myself, James," Mr. Waldruss replied, and turned to his neighbor. "What say you of your boy, Cotter?"

"Very well," Mr. Cotter said grudgingly. "But see you do not go beyond sound of my voice, young sir! I will have you at work the instant I call."

Simon looked as if he would leave his unfinished bread and meat to go along with them, but, "Oh, yes, sir, I will listen for you," Davy cried eagerly, and both boys jumped from the tree and ran pell-mell into the woods before Simon could follow.

"I don't know whether I detest Simon the more, or his evil father," Davy said when they were safely away. "But let us forget them, James, and be free men for a few minutes."

James had no great wish to be a freeman, because his situation was so good. Where else could a boy find a master like a kind father, a mistress as gentle as a mother, and four little girls who treated him exactly like an older brother? But he sympathized too much with Davy to say anything except, "Yes, let us explore, Davy!"

They walked through the trees, circling the clearing so as to remain within hearing of Mr. Cotter. The trees were tall, and the forest silent except for the low sounds of voices reaching them. They stood now where no man had stood for thousands of years, whispered Davy in a voice of awe.

"Save Indians," said James, and recalling, began to laugh, saying, "Remember how you promised me there were no more Indians?"

Davy joined him in the laughter, and said, "But in the way you meant, it is true. The few Indians between here and Boston are friendly as Christians."

Neither boy had as yet seen an Indian, and many years were to pass before they did.

They ventured a little farther to what seemed another clearing, from the shine of sun on snow. It was a small place with a great rise of rock. There was a shadowy space on the side of the hill. The boys approached cautiously, fearful a wild beast might spring out at them. There was no slightest sound, the world might have been holding its breath. The shadowy space was a cave opening, just as they had thought.

"I'm going to look within," whispered Davy, and when James protested the possible danger, Davy answered, "Oh, James, you don't know my feelings! What can a wild beast do to me that my master hasn't done already?"

"He might kill you!"

"And so may my master, one day," Davy said sadly. Both boys were whispering as much for protection against being heard by Simon as for fear of what the cave might hold.

Davy boldly bounded off, hesitated a moment at the mouth of the cave, then vanished into the shadows. In only a few seconds he was outside again, signaling eagerly for James to join him.

"It's a fine, dry cave," he whispered excitedly. "It will be ours, James, and none will know of it save us."

The cave may at one time have been the lair of a beast, but it was now clean and empty. The light reached only part of the way, but Davy said he had explored the wall all around with his hands.

"And now come. We must be back before Simon comes searching for us," Davy said eagerly. Outside he led the way back, not approaching the clearing directly from the cave, but following their own tracks all the way. "We don't want Simon, who is a great snoop, to follow a short trail of our footprints," Davy said, and then he added passionately, "It's ours, our very own, James. Promise you won't tell."

James promised. He did not feel the same excitement and joy as his friend, but he was boy enough to revel in a secret cave of his own, shared only with his dear friend.

After sap-time there came a great change in everyone's life, for now it was time to plow. The kind of work changed slowly with the weather. First the wooden plow with its iron share must be cleaned and the share sharpened that it might cut more easily through the earth. The yoke Mr. Waldruss had worked on all winter was finished and ready to bind his oxen into a team, but the harnesses must all be inspected and mended where mending was needed.

Mr. Waldruss was a kind of leader in the little settlement. It was he who went to visit the new German family. He took James along for, he said, "You must learn to deal with all."

The Schutters were agreeable, pleasant people who had come only a few months before. They seemed to have only one English word: "Eat, eat!" They offered spicy-smelling tarts so delicious that Mr. Waldruss finally had to say with a laugh, "Enough, James!" But he allowed the Germans to press two more on James, who obligingly gobbled them up.

It was interesting to James to hear the conversation that followed, and taught him how few words are needed for understanding.

"Oxen?" Mr. Waldruss asked, and Mr. Schutter held up four fingers.

"You have four oxen," Mr. Waldruss said, "and Cotter has four, and I have two. Ten will make a fine team, and can pull the plow even through your fresh-cleared land."

"*Ja, ja,*" said Mr. Schutter eagerly.

"Both sons can help?" Mr. Waldruss asked.

Again Mr. Schutter held up his fingers, two this time, and the two grown boys grinned and nodded enthusiastically. James grinned and nodded too, pleased as punch at how well everything was understood.

"Are they richer than we, sir?" he asked on the way

home. "Having four oxen to our two, and white sugar
for those cakies?"

"Yes, indeed," Mr. Waldruss said. "Far richer. He is
the relative of some German nobleman or other and came
here with money to buy land and beasts and tools. And,"
Mr. Waldruss sighed a little, "he has two grown sons."

James thought he heard regret in that sigh and said
quickly, "Sir, you have me! And I am growing! Mrs.
Waldruss has already had to let out my breeches, I
grow so fast."

"Aye, James," Mr. Waldruss agreed, laughing. "I have
you, and glad of it."

Before the ride was out James went on thoughtfully,
"Then Mr. Cotter must be richer than you, too, for he
has four oxen *and* a black slave."

For a long time Mr. Waldruss did not answer. Then
he said, "Yes, in money he is a man richer than I. I
do not envy Mr. Cotter, James. His meanness is something
I cannot abide. He gets his riches by a cruel kind of
thrift, saving on the very food he should give his slave
— and now, I doubt not, his bound boy. I do not enjoy
dealing with him, but in this wild country we cannot
always choose our neighbors. Like it or not, we must
all three work together to get our fields plowed in time
for seeding."

When they got back to the house, Mrs. Waldruss had
a store of questions for them. After she had cleared away
her curiosity as to all their plans, she asked, "And their

elder son? The one they call Hans? Has he spoken for Annie Beadle yet?"

Mr. Waldruss gave an impatient exclamation. "What are you thinking of? Spoken for Annie indeed! How can he speak for her when the only word of English he seems to know is *eat*?"

"Mark my words," Mrs. Waldruss said with a knowing smile. "I watch them in church, you see. My word for it, they'll be a match."

"I don't know how it is to be, then, unless someone speaks for young Schutter, who certainly cannot speak for himself."

"Ah, he has asked you to speak for him, then," Mrs. Waldruss said complacently. "I thought he would. You are beyond compare the very man to carry his plea."

Mr. Waldruss' face grew so red with exasperation that James, always ready to be frightened, poised himself for flight. A small silence followed, during which Mrs. Waldruss, completely unaware of the storm in her husband, went about her work looking pleased and satisfied.

"Listen to me, now," her husband began, so mildly that James was astonished. He was not used to anger that could be controlled or diverted. "I am no cupid for Hans Schutter. I have heard no word of Annie Beadle from him. I went there today to arrange for the plowing and did so. James went to fill himself with cakies, and he did so. More we did not do."

"Oh, did you not, then?" Mrs. Waldruss asked with

her unfailing good humor. "Well, you will be asked in time. Do not grow impatient."

"There is no fear of that," Mr. Waldruss said with equal good humor and took up a piece of wood and a knife. Mr. Waldruss was a steady whittler. James could not help but wonder now if some of the whittling might not be Mr. Waldruss' method of dealing with his wife's nonsense. Anyone with a knife in his hand might safely be angry at a piece of wood.

Chapter 9

Time to Plow

In the silent dark before dawn, they hitched all the oxen to a two-coultered plow. They started in Schutter's fields. The German's plow was, like all the others, principally of wood, but it had been reinforced with iron purchased from the foundry in Saugus. The coulters were of iron entirely, like two sturdy teeth.

Mr. Waldruss dealt out the labors: "Cotter will guide plow, and I will ride plow. Schutter will go after with his hack, digging where we leave great clods. Catto will go before in case of stones, the lads with him."

Mr. Waldruss sat himself down on the plow, that his great weight would give more purchase to the share and help turn the hard-packed ground that had never before known the tool of man. The oxen, straining at their chains, made their first furrow — none too straight against the

85

solid ground! — and came back down the field again in
the same unsteady way. Schutter's new fields were full
of the stump holes where the hardworking Germans had
been able to dig out the roots of the trees they had
felled, and there were plenty of stumps still stubbornly
standing.

It was hard work for the boys, even with a strong
boy like Catto to help, digging out the stones that might
injure the plow. Hans and Wilhelm Schutter, the sons,
worked with a will. They always had a smile when
James looked their way. Catto was a silent, willing worker, as were James and Davy, but Simon Cotter was bent
on mischief — and worse.

He always called James "bound-boy" when they were
alone. And invariably he called Davy, "Scum!" Now, as
they came to the end of Schutter's last furrow in the
fading sunlight, he inquired how James had fared at his
last lashing.

"He's never been lashed!" Davy said.

"I have a kind master," James retorted indignantly.

"You will be lashed, though, and worse," Simon promised. "A bondsman in Boston struck his master and had
his ears cut off, and so will you, one day soon."

"Oh, master! You fright the lad!" Catto protested.

"You'd better be frightened yourself," Simon said arrogantly, "or I'll have my father treat you like a white
slave. You won't like that, will you?"

"No, master," Catto said humbly and said no more,
with only kind, pitying looks for James and Davy.

"Black slaves must be cared for, to give a lifetime of service," Simon said arrogantly. "White slaves may be worked till they drop, to get the good out of them before their time is out. And they must be brought to heel, or — "

"Cotter, see to your son!" roared Mr. Waldruss, who had come on them unheard. He put a strong, reassuring arm about James. "Simon's been frightening my boy out of his wits, and Davy — poor Catto, too, if I'm any judge!"

Cotter said mildly, "Now, Simon." Mr. Waldruss wait-

ed, as if for more from Mr. Cotter, but it soon became
clear he had had his say. Mr. Waldruss then went on
very kindly, "There are bad servants and cruel masters,
James, but I hope you and I will never earn the name
of one or the other."

James was doubly touched, once with gratitude for
his master's kindness, again with pity for the desperate
look on Davy's face.

The new fields plowed, the farmers went on to finish
the others. This was accomplished quickly, for the soil
that had been turned before answered easily to the plow
this time. When at last the plowing was done, each man
returned to his own farm.

"Now we must prepare the earth for the seed," Mr.
Waldruss said.

Now all, even Mrs. Waldruss, went into the fields daily.
Mr. and Mrs. Waldruss worked with hoes and rakes.
Small saplings were cut down, and James and the older
girls dragged them over the turned ground to smooth
it. Then at last it was time to put in the seeds.

Their biggest crop was corn. They used it for flour and
porridge and fodder for the beasts. The dried cobs were
used for kindling. All they did not need could be sold
in a ready market.

They planted pumpkins and beans. A small field each
they sowed to wheat and barley.

"I hardly hope for much with the barley," Mr. Waldruss explained to Davy, "and rarely get even as good
as I hope for."

In New England the barley grew poor. "It comes coarse, making the poorest kind of malt liquor," Mr. Waldruss added. Still there was enough of a barley crop to make the family ale each year. James, who never touched ale now that he could have all the milk he wanted, could still recognize the need for the drink that seemed to answer his master's every wish in a beverage. In winter ale warmed his master and in the summer cooled him.

There was a kitchen garden for greens and roots, and one corner here Mr. Waldruss set apart for an oddity he planted each year. "It is a vegetable much valued by the Indians," he told James, "and is called a potato."

Mr. Waldruss sowed potatoes each year, and the family would enjoy the small yield, roasting them in the ashes. Rarely were any carried to market. Mr. Waldruss found potatoes very flavorsome and was sure that someday they would make a money crop. "But that day has not yet come," he would decide each year.

Chapter 10

To Boston for Boots

The days after plowing and sowing were busy. James and Mr. Waldruss were in the fields all day now, from sunup to sundown. Meals of bread and roasted meats were brought to them by Hitty. Elizabeth could not be spared — she must work side by side with her mother. No day was too long, no task too hard for James when Mr. Waldruss said, "Good work, boy."

Enough flax was grown for the family needs, and at least half of its culture made work for the children. Each did her share about the farm. Even little Rachel could help with the weeding, and tiny Mary clapped the wooden bird-scarer industriously.

Mrs. Waldruss and the older girls were never finished with their spinning and weaving and sewing and knitting. Rarely was pretty little Hitty to be seen without her nimble fingers busy at the tiny loom on which she wove the tapes that were used as boot strings, stay laces, belts, and breeches suspenders.

The summer sped into autumn, and then there were nuts to gather and wild fruits. They made trips to the seashore for clams and mussels.

James lived such days as he had never dreamed could come to him. Kindness and plenty surrounded him.

"My boy, how you grow!" Mr. Waldruss exclaimed when Mrs. Waldruss complained that there was no way to increase the size of his clothes and that she must make him a new outfit cut to his measure.

James, who had been mostly unaware of his growth, thought what a strange thing it was that his concern over being undersized had vanished. He rarely considered it now, although once it had been a great trouble to him. Before it had been one more thing to be unhappy about. Now, with all the goodness surrounding him, his size seemed of no matter at all. What if he did after all end up as a small man? He had learned that there were more important things than mere size. And yet, since he had grown in the time he had been bound to Mr. Waldruss and since his master had remarked on that growth, he wanted to thank him.

"It must be all this good food," he said. "Perhaps I am not to be so small after all."

"Indeed, and you promise to be tall!" Mr. Waldruss said with surprise.

Cousin Beadle's shallop was busy now, hauling corn and wheat and eggs and cheeses to Boston. Mr. Waldruss and James would load the cart high, and then Mr. Waldruss would go off, the long way around by the cart road through the meadows and along the shore, to load it all into the shallop. Cousin Beadle would pitch in with him, and Mr. Waldruss paid for his labor and the use of his boat by giving him corn for Annie's hens, or a suckling pig, or a cheese from the load he carried.

James wished he could go along, but he did not ask and knew it could not be. The shallop was a small boat and rode low in the water when she was so heavily laden. There was room for nothing more, not even a boy.

Mr. Waldruss explained that Cousin Beadle did a thriving business as a drayboatsman for the few weeks after the harvest and then again later, after killing-time, when there was meat to bring to market too.

"Cotter and Schutter use him as well," Mr. Waldruss concluded. "It is a good addition to his fishing business."

One day when there was no cargo for Cousin Beadle, Mr. Waldruss said, "James, I must get my hoe from the blacksmith in Boston. He has had a pretty weight of corn from me for the job. You must have new boots against the winter, and the best bootmaker is in Boston."

James hugged himself with joy. They rode double on the horse through the flame-tinted woods and came to Cousin Beadle's to find other horses and an air of excitement. The Schutters were there, and the Cotters — and Davy! All had small errands to do in Boston — at the cooper's, or the blacksmith's, or the shops. For Davy and Simon there would be a trip to the bootmaker's, also.

"They are too hard on their boots," Mr. Cotter grumbled.

Annie came out to help with the horses, and James was able to observe her and Hans. They did not once look at one another. In fact if Annie was near the barn, Hans immediately walked to the duckpond. Did Annie walk to the jetty? Hans found business with his horse.

"It does seem Mrs. Waldruss may have been mistaken," James whispered to his master after much careful observation. "They seem rather to avoid one another."

"You've noticed it, have you?" his master said with a chuckle. "Aye, they do seem to dislike one another, but I fear me a woman's eyes are sharper than ours. There is too much looking away, James. Mark it well. Now that Mrs. Waldruss has opened my eyes, I can predict they will be married by spring."

James had hardly time to try to understand this when something else attracted his attention and that of everyone else. Mr. Waldruss handed Cousin Beadle two shillings, saying loudly, "A shilling a head, hard cash."

The Schutters took the hint at once, and there being three of them — young Wilhelm was along too — Mr. Schutter dropped three shillings into Cousin Beadle's eager hands.

There was a long pause while everyone looked at Mr. Cotter.

"I have a little pig at home for you, Beadle," Mr. Cotter said persuasively.

"Keep your pig at home, and stay there with him," Cousin Beadle said. "All aboard that's paid fare," he sang out, barring the way against the Cotter party.

'Don't you need some geese?" Cotter persisted, "As handsome a pair of geese as ever you saw."

"It's me you think a goose," Cousin Beadle said contemptuously. "Hard cash for this pleasure trip, or no trip."

James looked anxiously at Davy, who had his hands gripped tight together as if to defend against showing his feelings.

"Come on, Cotter, yes or no," Mr. Waldruss called out impatiently. Mr. Cotter hesitated only briefly, then dropped two shillings into Cousin Beadle's hand.

"Three," Cousin Beadle said.

"You demand fare for a white slave?" Mr. Cotter asked indignantly.

"White slave or green slave, he takes the same space as any other human," Cousin Beadle said. "Last call."

"Do you realize I will have to lay out more cash to the bootmaker? This great hulk of a boy has outgrown his boots!"

"Worn them out too, by the looks of them," Mr. Waldruss said. "He's as stubborn as my James, who in spite of my direct orders has persisted in growing too large for his boots, and wearing through the soles besides. We are hard-used men, Cotter, to have healthy boys who work so hard they wear out their boots and grow big and strong only to be able to do more work and wear out more boots. I commiserate with you."

"Ah, I know your jokes," Mr. Cotter grumbled and parted with his third shilling.

They filed aboard, making nine in all. Annie stood and waved them off, carefully looking at her father, or the mast, or the prow. If she liked Hans Schutter, she had a queer way of showing it, James decided and then forgot Annie as Davy began slowly to move toward him, and he toward Davy, so that they finally met amidships and sat down together.

"Fancy our going to Boston for boots!" Davy remarked airily, with a look of great enjoyment. James marvelled at his ability to take pleasure when it came, rather than allow the general misery of his life to cast him down forever.

There was no question of Davy's bad treatment. One had only to look at him. He was ill dressed for the trip, in a shameful mass of rags. He was thin to gauntness, and he looked in general overworked and underfed; yet he could act like a great lord because he was going to Boston for boots.

When they docked in Boston to go their separate ways, there was talk about the time to be set for their return. The only clock Cousin Beadle knew of was the one with chimes at the Dockside Inn, and it was agreed that they would meet there at four by that clock.

"And be there," Cousin Beadle instructed. "I'm not

way. They were too shy to go inside by themselves. Mr. Waldruss peered inside at the clock, said, "It is only two o'clock, and I am hungry. We've all missed our nooning."

The Schutters, when they had been made to understand, were eager and kept nodding their heads and saying cheerfully, "Eat, eat." Even Mr. Cotter unwillingly

granted that it would be many hours yet before they would be home. The men being all agreed, they started in. Cotter called out to Davy, "Wait quietly outside."

Mr. Waldruss and James stopped short, although the Schutters, probably from not understanding, continued into the pleasant dimness of the inn.

"Come, Cotter, your boy must be just as hungry as we are," Mr. Waldruss protested.

"Let him wait. There's good food enough at home for him, and this all costs. This will be all for cash, you know, no barter."

"If James will agree to eat modestly, I believe I can afford to have Davy as my guest," Mr. Waldruss said with a sigh. James understood that sigh and honored his master for it. Mr. Waldruss was open in his talk of money, and James knew how few shillings there really were to spend.

"The more fool you," Mr. Cotter said and joined the Schutters at the plank table in the center of the room. James ran outside and got Davy, and by the time they joined the others, the Schutters had learned the truth from Mr. Cotter himself. He had no inconvenient shame on the subject. By signs and half words and smiles, Mr. Schutter showed his insistence upon paying for half of Davy's meal. Mr. Waldruss accepted cheerfully, saying, "Then in that case we may all eat well."

They ordered bread and meat and a new beverage they had heard of called tea. The tea was served hot and some sugar with it, and all declared it a delicious

drink. All three men purchased packets of the tea and
got directions for its preparation. Even Mr. Cotter did not
begrudge the expense. He agreed with the others that
it had an excellent chance of becoming popular in time.

Chapter 11

Davy Pleads for Help

For James, the summer now flown had had only one blight, the sorrow that came to him through seeing Davy so ill used. When they saw one another at church, it was only to exchange glances. Mr. Cotter hurried Davy home immediately, as if to put him back to work, Sabbath or no Sabbath, as speedily as possible. On those rare occasions when they spoke, Davy confessed he was not given enough to eat and that his treatment was otherwise harsh.

"Not cruel, I hope," James said earnestly.

"No, unless you count it cruel to beat down the spirit and degrade all hope. Oh, James, how glad I am for the good of your place! You could not stand in my shoes without my strength and my will."

There came a day when even Davy could not stand it. It was a cold November day when the killing of the beasts was about to start. All slaughtering was done in the late fall, to insure that the meat would not spoil before it could be smoked or salted.

"You are still too small to do any part of this job," Mr. Waldruss said, "but you must watch me and learn as best you can."

James did not overmuch like the prospect of watching the killing, but always obedient to the man he now loved like a father, he took his place by Mr. Waldruss' side.

They started first with a sheep, for mutton was to be one of their foods. When they were almost to the shed

they saw, off in the distance, someone half staggering, half running. Going forward to meet him, they soon saw it was Davy, dressed poorly for the day in only a shirt and breeches. He almost fell into Mr. Waldruss' arms, and then James saw the shirt had been ripped across by the lash. His friend's back was cut and bleeding.

"Come, now, Davy, do not fear," said Mr. Waldruss. "And you, James, leave off your gawking and go on his other side that he may lean on you."

Walking thus, they soon reached the house. Mrs. Waldruss gave a sharp scream on first seeing Davy, but soon showed that in emergencies she was no one to trifle with. She washed Davy's wounds in the gentlest manner and salved them with the raccoon grease she kept for such purposes. Davy, still silent — he had not uttered one single word since he fell into Mr. Waldruss' arms — gritted his teeth and did not let a sound escape him.

"A cruel, cruel thing," Mrs. Waldruss said as she worked. "And Davy so good a boy."

"Aye, and I'm not a bad one," Davy said unexpectedly. "For being insolent, he said. My bond, sir, if I spoke an insolent word."

"This cannot be allowed," Mr. Waldruss said. "I will send word to my neighbor Cotter to meet us at the Magistrate's in Boston as soon as Davy can travel."

But before he could plan more, Davy had fainted. Mr. Waldruss lifted him up as easy as if he were a baby and carried him to the bed by the fire. He stood look-

ing down at the unconscious boy for a long time, then
said gravely, "Care for him. I'll go to Cotter myself."

James heard with foreboding the hoofs of his horse
clatter off and went to stand by Davy, who was now
moaning but still not conscious.

"Oh, ma'am," James said fearfully, and Mrs. Waldruss
replied, "He will be well. It will take only time to see
him fully recovered."

James pulled a three-legged stool over by the bed
and sat down. Soon after, they heard horses, more than
one, and in came Mr. Waldruss with Mr. Cotter.

"Where is the rogue?" he cried out angrily, and Mr.
Waldruss pointed silently to the bed. Mr. Cotter would
have grasped and shaken Davy but that Mr. Waldruss
put out a great restraining hand. "He must have time
to recover and good care, Cotter. And if you fail to give
me your word not to deal with him so again, it's the
Magistrate in Boston will fix it."

James could see that Mr. Cotter did not want to make
the promise, but it was clear he feared Mr. Waldruss'
displeasure more than the defeat of not having his own
way. After a moment he muttered, "Yes, then, since you
will have a promise. But he must mend his ways too
and mind his words to his master."

When he learned that Mr. Waldruss did not mean to
allow Davy to be moved until he was recovered, Mr.
Cotter was again ready for argument. Then suddenly
he interrupted himself to say, "Yes, very well, he may
stay till he can work again. But it is all by your wish,

look you. I'll not pay a penny for his keep, since you are so set on being his keeper."

He left the house still raging, and as if hearing him go, Davy roused himself and asked, "Will we go to the Magistrate, then?"

"No need," said Mr. Waldruss and told what had passed.

"He's a liar," said Davy. "But if he gives his word, and if he fears you, then he may keep it."

"And you will stay here until your wounds are healed," said James joyfully. He could have asked for nothing more, except perhaps that Davy might stay forever.

He and Mr. Waldruss now went back outside about the business that Davy had interrupted.

Later a second pallet was hastily laid down next to James's, and after their evening bread and milk the boys went upstairs, Davy slowly and painfully.

"I wish you could always be here," James whispered.

"I could pray for nothing better," Davy said, adding sadly, "but it is not to be."

The next day there were a steer and a great hog to kill. While James went with his master, Davy stayed indoors, stiff and hardly moving for the pain of his wounds. Once, when James ran in for water for the whetstone so Mr. Waldruss could sharpen his knives, Davy said, "If I had a piece of wood it would help pass the time of day."

James brought in a piece of maple from the woodpile,

and with Mr. Waldruss' permission, one of the sharpened knives. Thereafter Davy busied himself whittling,
seeming quite content. At the end of only two days he
had a handsome ladle carved out of the wood.

"You are an artisan with a knife," Mr. Waldruss said,
taking up the ladle and turning it this way and that to
admire it.

"I wish Mrs. Waldruss to have it, for her kind care
of me," said Davy.

Mr. Waldruss gently put the ladle back into Davy's
hands. "It is not yours to give, Davy boy. What you
make is your master's. It will have to be given to him."

"Is this true?" Davy asked sharply. On Mr. Waldruss'
assurance that there was no choice in the matter, Davy
took the ladle, snapped it into two pieces across his
knee, and threw it into the fire. "That for my master
Cotter."

"I do not blame you, Davy," James said loyally, and
Mr. Waldruss, sighing, said, "No, nor do I. But be a
good boy, Davy, and do your work, and I doubt not
your trouble is past."

In another day Mr. Cotter came and got Davy, saying
he was ready for light work. James so much disliked his
going that it emboldened him to say, as he and Mr.
Waldruss watched them leave, "Sir, I wish you were his
master too."

"I wish anyone were, save Cotter," said Mr. Waldruss.

Chapter 12

James Goes to A Party

Life on the Waldruss farm was a serious and steady thing. All winter long wood had to be chopped in great loads, otherwise the cold must have won the grim battle. Water must be fetched from the spring each day and kept by the fire so it would not freeze as it might if it were set in that part of the room where no heat reached.

In all his free time, Mr. Waldruss went to whittling. It was he who had made all the trenchers the household used, although other woodenware, like the buckets, he had bought from the cooper. At first James could not wait to get his hands on a sharp knife and a piece of wood, yet when at last he did so he found it a slow, tedious task and not at all to his liking.

Other work about the farm he enjoyed, even to cleaning out the stalls. He would work in great contentment, often alone, getting satisfaction out of contributing to the comfort of the beasts. The horse would nudge him in greeting, and the cows would give a soft low. The two oxen were so placid they never stopped their munching. James talked to them gently as he worked, smiling inwardly whenever an animal seemed to make a sound he could take for an answer.

He still thought of himself as a creature of fears, but had the consolation of knowing that it was a secret he shared with no one. He had long understood that he had nothing to fear from anyone in the Waldruss family, and that gave him the power to handle himself when he was fearful — in the presence of Mr. Cotter, for instance, or sometimes walking out to the barn in the night on an errand for his master.

James never ceased to marvel at his new life. He was part of a family, because the Waldrusses treated him as one of themselves. They had become the whole of his life. Everything that had happened to him in his first twelve years — the neglect, the brutality, the near starvation — all had vanished into a single sour memory he called England. His real life was here, all its concerns were his. Never did he realize it so clearly as when Mrs. Waldruss' suspicions of Hans Schutter and Annie Beadle proved real. James was as gleeful as his mistress.

"So he has asked you to speak for him?" Mrs. Waldruss said to her husband. "Well, I'm not surprised. I always said he would."

"But what words could Hans use?" James asked. "He knows no English. He could not say, 'Marry me.'"

"Time has taught him much. And besides," Mr. Waldruss added drily, "only a few words are enough when a man is determined to marry. He said Annie's name and made it clear, brokenly it is true, but still clear, that he wished me to speak to Cousin Beadle for him. Well, I see nothing against it. The Schutters are good people, and Annie's getting on — she's near eighteen. James and I will go tomorrow to dig for clams, and I will take the opportunity to speak to my Cousin Beadle then."

James was delighted to be part of such a family affair and listened greedily next day while the two men talked.

"Aye, I know," Cousin Beadle said at once. "I've watched him making sheep's eyes at my Annie. I knew it had to come. Well, I'll make no objection and hope he'll make none about taking me along with my daughter."

Mr. Waldruss said he would pass the message on to Hans. He explained to James that ordinarily Hans would himself have spoken to Cousin Beadle, but that his limited English had made this seem the better way. "Besides, it is easier for me to settle it about Cousin Beadle living with them, for how else is my cousin to live, with no woman to keep house for him?"

"But is Annie herself not to be consulted?"

"Ah, my boy, I am sure that Hans has made himself clear to Annie and that she has shown herself willing. Else Hans would not have gone so far as to send me to her father."

No difficulties were made by the Schutters. They seemed to appreciate Hans's good fortune in having a house ready to move into, and in their broken English conveyed that they foresaw nothing but happiness for the young couple.

"Then Hans will be our cousin by marriage, sir?" James asked on the way home.

"And one I welcome." Mr. Waldruss smiled down at James as at some secret joke, but it was not until James was on his pallet, drifting off, that he understood that smile. "Our cousin," he had said, as if he were indeed a Waldruss! And Mr. Waldruss, beyond that knowing smile, had offered no protest! James fell the rest of the way into contented sleep.

The banns were called for Annie and Hans on three Sundays, and then they were married, she in a neat gray cotton gown of her own make. The families were invited to Cousin Beadle's for cakes and ale, and James was one of the family as surely as if the same blood ran in his veins.

He was a happy boy. As always, the only sadness that came to him was seeing the misery of Davy. Mr. Cotter had not again beaten him, but Davy worked too hard with too little food to sustain him, and only Simon's castoff rags to wear. They met to talk and be together at second sap-time, when they again ran off to see that their cave was safe and still untenanted. Apart from that, James, riding on the cart with his master as they went to the shore to fish or clam, would sometimes catch a glimpse of poor Davy, carrying a load heavy enough for two men or drudging late and early.

"Sir, could you buy Davy from Mr. Cotter?" he finally found the courage to ask.

Mr. Waldruss shook his head. "I've offered for him, James," he said. "But I have nothing Cotter wants. The man won't listen to reason. He asks thirty pounds, determined to bleed me for my compassion. I haven't the money for it. I have a family and a boy of my own to care for, and hard money is a scarce thing for a farmer!"

James knew that a price of thirty pounds was only Mr. Cotter's cruel way of refusing to sell Davy. Again he sighed for his friend.

Another year passed, and sap-time came once more. The two boys met again, James with a joyful greeting, Davy more reserved now. They had both grown, Davy in spite of his poor treatment, James probably because of all the food and love that came his way. Davy was a head taller than his master, and James, surprisingly, already reached to Mr. Waldruss' shoulders.

"Remember what a baby you were?" Davy asked sadly after they had inspected their cave and were on their way back to the others. "And now you are a fine good size."

He spoke so gravely, so unlike a boy of sixteen, that James burst out, "Oh, Davy, is it so bad?"

"I believe I can continue to bear it," Davy said with the old proud lift of his head. "But, oh, James, I count the days."

"If only there was something — "

"There is nothing. Nothing." Davy spoke with the sureness of resignation, and there was time for no more. They were back to the sugar clearing.

It was shortly after sugaring-time that Annie and Hans Schutter's child was born. It was a son, to be called by the English translation of Hans into John.

The infant was seen in church when he was four days old. It was the custom to baptize all infants on the Sunday immediately following their birth, no matter how inclement the weather, to make sure of salvation in case of the early death which carried off so many infants. The April morning was stormy, with sleet and ice, and James, who took a close interest in his new little "cousin," protested that baptism could have waited a week or more. "He is such a mite to brave the storm," he said. "He may yet die of his baptism."

But there was no danger of little John dying, storm or no storm. He screamed healthily at the first drop of water from the minister's hand.

"A lusty boy," agreed the Waldrusses, who stood godparents.

The three grandparents looked as proud as grandparents usually look, and the elder Schutters said there would be a christening party at their house.

Apart from Annie's quiet wedding, James had never been to a party. When the great evening came, he went with a curiosity and eagerness not equalled by even the littlest Waldruss girl; all the children came along as a matter of course.

The Schutter house was snug against the cool night and full of the young new family and the old. There were more to come. Several of the inland families had been invited.

"And Cotter will be here with Simon and his wife and daughters," Schutter said, and thoughts of seeing Davy intensified James's excitement all the more. He soon saw that a party meant wooden platters of sliced meat to eat and the sweets he called cakies, and egg cakes and macaroons and watered wine for the children, with something a little stronger for the grownups.

There were not enough of the family trenchers to go around, so everything was to be eaten directly from the platter, with only fingers as utensils. There was one two-tined pewter fork that Mrs. Schutter handed about as a great curiosity. She demonstrated its use by lifting a piece of meat with it.

"I will whittle us a few of those," Mr. Waldruss said. "They seem to be useful things and may come in handy in many ways."

James had hardly got through a first sampling of ev-

erything when a wonderful surprise was announced.
They were to have music! Old Mr. Schutter produced a
fiddle and ran his bow across the strings, then called
out that there would be dancing for the young people
while the elders watched.

"No refusals accepted," Annie cried and went about
the room, pairing the couples.

The Schutters all joined her in urging the shy and giving demonstrations. James found himself with his right

foot forward, ready to start the dance with Hitty at his side. Elizabeth was partnered by Simon Cotter, who came just in time for the dance.

"As near as I can make out, we are to hop and skip and whirl about," James whispered anxiously to Hitty. She had grown too in the three years past and was a pretty girl of a good height, very much attached to James and with a lively spirit of great independence.

Thus she answered him confidently, "Oh, a great deal of whirling about," as if she knew the dance well. "It is a German dance, you see," she added, as if this explained all.

The music started and they hopped, skipped, and whirled about, repeating it so often and with such an enthusiastic disregard for their neighbors, that there was also a great deal of bumping into one another and apologizing and laughter. When the music stopped they were eager for more, asking only time to fetch breath and begin again. A window was opened to cool the room, and laughing gasps could be heard throughout.

It was while they were resting that James looked about for Davy, finally appealing to Simon.

"That scum? He's out in the barn where he belongs. He's fit to drive the cart, that we might sit on clean straw, but the Cotter servant doesn't come to the party."

James returned to Hitty as the fiddle struck up and went through this dance with a reserve and gravity ill suited to its tempo.

"What is wrong, James?" Hitty asked as soon as the

music stopped. He told her, and she called Elizabeth to her side and repeated it. The three young people stood looking at one another in great resentment and anger.

There was to be a rest now between dances so that more of Mrs. Schutter's good food could be disposed of and more of Mr. Schutter's good wine drunk. James watched his chance and took a trencher from the cupboard. With the connivance of the girls, he piled it high with food. There was so much bustle and noise that he went unnoticed as he slipped from the room.

There was a full moon overhead to see by — the Schutters had of course planned their party for a moonlight night — and he made his way quietly to the barn. He was balancing the trencher in one hand and a mug in the other. He kicked lightly on the barn door. Davy opened it instantly. He had been sitting with the beasts in the dark.

"James — is it you, James?" he asked. Davy's voice had none of its old bright sparkle, and James surmised that at least part of his friend's depression was caused by the sounds of gaiety within and his distress at having no part in it. His guess was borne out by Davy's instant response to his: "James here, Davy Butcher!"

"A welcome to you, James," he said with a beginning of cheerfulness.

"And what is your pleasure?" James went on. "Will it be meat or cakies or wine?"

Davy snatched up a slice of meat, gobbled it down, and said, "I have not seen this much food since I set foot in America. James, James, you are a good friend to me."

They sat together, hardly speaking while Davy finished to the last crumb. Then James took the trencher and mug and hastened back, hoping he had not been missed.

The girls looked at the empty dishes and smiled triumphantly. A new dance was being got up, and James again took his place, the girls theirs, and they whirled about together with happier hearts.

Later it was the older people's turn to dance, and the young ones must watch. Hans played a tolerable fiddle too, so his parents and the Waldrusses, Cousin Beadle and a Cotter daughter, Mr. and Mrs. Cotter, and the other guests took their turn.

The room became very full, and James snatched at this opportunity to refill the trencher and mug and, this time accompanied by the girls, went back to Davy.

Davy obligingly did away with the new supply of food. After that, the music from within sounding clear through the open window, Elizabeth and Hitty determined that Davy must learn the German dance. Before another minute had passed, the four of them were hopping, skipping, and whirling freely about the yard. Davy was as full of joy as any of them.

"So here you are!" Simon snapped out.

They stopped short, in midwhirl.

"I'd have thought you had more pride, Elizabeth," Simon jeered.

James had observed with some concern Simon's growing partiality for Elizabeth. He was too fond of her as
a sister to be willing to see her attach herself to a Cotter. Now his mind was set at rest as she replied, "I have
great pride in my friends Davy and James."

Simon turned and walked away angrily. The girls
hastily retrieved the trencher and mug and ran inside.

"I won't leave you to bear it alone," Davy said
staunchly. "I'll go inside and claim the blame."

James would have none of it. "My master will smooth
it over, you will see," he promised, although inwardly
he trembled. He did not feel he had done wrong, as Mr.
Waldruss would see wrong, but there was Mr. Cotter
to consider too. Mr. Cotter was a rich man, made important in that small community by his riches. Who
could tell what power he might have to harm his master?

When he reached the house it was clear the Cotters
had already been told by Simon, and that Mr. Cotter had
something to say on the subject.

"So," he said to James, "you have been stealing your
host's food, have you?"

Annie, coming into the room with a fresh dish of
sweets, seemed to catch his meaning instantly, and she
was a girl of spirit. "Did you not know," she asked,
"that it was Father Schutter who sent James out with
the food for your boy? We could see you had forgot
poor Davy. We didn't wish to trouble you over it. Has
the boy had enough, James?"

"Quite enough," James said gratefully.

"Then we may go on with the party," Mrs. Waldruss said in her comfortable way. "Mr. Cotter, you have no need to fret yourself. Davy has been fed, and your worry was all for nothing."

"Aye, Cotter, you are a worrier," Mr. Waldruss said. "You see how matters right themselves when left to run their natural course."

The party did go on after that, in spite of Mr. Cotter's purple face and Simon's surly looks.

Chapter 13

Davy Disappears

It was not long after the beginning of the new year that Mr. Cotter came riding up one afternoon, just as Mr. Waldruss and James were leaving the house to fetch firewood. Mr. Cotter jumped angrily to the ground, crushing the frozen snow.

"Have you any word of my boy?" he asked in a rage. He turned more particularly to James to add, "Your scoundrelly friend!"

James's heart gave a great triumphant lurch within him. He's got away, he thought. He had often told himself that in Davy's place he would have run away long ago.

"Sir, we have not seen Davy," he said, faltering because he was always afraid of Mr. Cotter, even with his master standing by. As he spoke it seemed to him that he caught a flicker of motion from among the trees in the distance. The day was dark and overcast, but still he was sure he saw someone or something move. It must be Davy! Purposely he turned about so that he would not seem to be looking in that direction.

His little trick did him no good. Mr. Cotter had caught the same flicker and was off on his horse in an instant. James stood watching, his heart sinking as horse and rider vanished into the woods.

"I'm sorry for Davy," Mr. Waldruss said gravely. "Cotter will surely catch him — a man on a horse against a boy on foot!"

"Oh, sir!" James could only get the two words out before the lump in his throat grew too great for talking.

"It will be hard on Davy now," Mr. Waldruss said. "The law is strict about runaways."

James, who until now had not even noticed the cold, suddenly felt a chill reach to his very bones. A faint sifting of flakes came ominously drifting down. "Oh, sir, what can we do?" he choked out.

Mr. Waldruss looked at him kindly, seeming to see the terror in James's heart.

"I can promise nothing," Mr. Waldruss said. "But I will ride to Cotter's tomorrow, the first minute I can get away."

"I can care for the beasts and get the water. Sir, will you go at sunrise?"

Mr. Waldruss did not laugh, as James had half ex-

pected him to, but nodded solemnly in a promise. "I
would go this very night," he said, "if there were a moon
to light my way. But it gets dark already."

This added both to James's comfort and to his terror.
Although he felt consoled to think his master was going
to speak for his friend, his manner, so serious and with
an air almost of foreboding, frightened him.

They went indoors now, because the cold had become
too intense to bear as the last of the sun vanished. The
snow was still only a sifting, but it added to their dis-
comfort. James, picking over his plentiful supper, had
to keep blinking back tears.

"Bless me, the boy's sick!" Mrs. Waldruss exclaimed
at seeing his food hardly touched.

"Sick at heart," Mr. Waldruss said. "As I am. As anyone would be." He explained what had transpired with
Davy, Mrs. Waldruss kept saying, "Oh, mercy, mercy!"

Elizabeth burst into frantic tears, and the two young-
est girls, understanding only that their older sister wept,
wailed loudly in company. Hitty alone remained dry-
eyed.

"Were I only a man," she said in a voice that trembled
with her indignation, "or were I only a woman large
enough to give Mr. Cotter back a taste — "

"That is enough, Hitty," Mrs. Waldruss said firmly.
"We'll have no ungodly talk of revenge. Revenge is the
Lord's. And in addition you are a girl, and must not
talk of fighting. It is not ladylike." Mrs. Waldruss said

all this with absent-minded solemnity, then burst out, "Oh, poor Davy. That dreadful man Cotter!"

"I would have my father go and lay Mr. Cotter flat with a single blow, as he easily could," Hitty stormed. "Go, sir, and rescue Davy."

James heard little of what the Waldrusses now cried out to admonish Hitty against harboring such thoughts. He was all in sympathy with her sentiments, and had only just finished wishing that he were strong enough to defend Davy by any means whatever.

He had his first uneasy night in that house, hovering between a natural will to sleep and an uneasy listening, waiting for he knew not what.

There was no need for anyone to wake him that morning. He was up before the first cold ray of the sun, up and dressed and out to the barn in his eagerness to show how well his master could be spared.

Mr. Waldruss was as good as his word. The sun was barely full up when he set out on the horse James had already saddled. It was not a long ride to Cotter's farm in an ordinary way; but the snow had settled into a steady storm, and this would slow the horse. James, watching him out of sight, calculated with a sigh that the sun would be high before he saw Mr. Waldruss once more. He set to work again, determined that his master's kindness should be repaid as far as could be with contented beasts and firewood in plenty.

The snow began to ease off, having put down a layer

two feet deep and drifts higher than a man's head. While the family sat over a hot meal of stew, there came the neigh of a horse, and James sprang to his feet. He flung open the door to admit his master.

"It's a bitter day," were Mr. Waldruss' first words. Catching sight of James, he added, "I wish I bore good news, boy."

James swallowed hard and stared horrified at his master. Mr. Waldruss took off his mittens and then his jacket, walking about, stamping the blood back into his feet. "Cotter caught Davy as we thought he might, and he must have beaten him sore. The law gives him that right — but I fear me he went too far. He left him lying in the barn after his beating, and this morning the boy was gone again."

"Good!" James burst out almost gaily.

"Alas, James, you don't stop to think!" Mr. Waldruss said. "Where is this poor beaten boy? The snow did him the kindness of hiding his tracks, but it is still a storm of snow. In this bitter cold, and with nothing to wear but his shirt and breeches — ?" He shook his head sadly. "Cotter said he would not trouble to seek Davy, which makes me fear the beating was very bad indeed. It seemed to me that Cotter thought he might die of it anyway, storm or no storm."

"He will come here," James said.

"If he lives," Mr. Waldruss said. "James, you forget my horse."

James recalled himself and went promptly to stable

the horse. Afterward he walked around the barn slowly, looking as far as his eye could reach. No living thing moved in all that white space. *He is hiding among the trees, then,* Davy told himself, but he knew that nobody could live the day out in that bitter cold without shelter and, particularly, hurt as Davy must have been. *Then he will surely come here,* James promised himself, and still slowly, still seeking, he walked back to the house.

When Mr. Waldruss had warmed up and got the cold out of his bones, he and Davy walked over the frozen snow, going to a nearby hill and getting a clear view of the country roundabout.

"He is not to be seen," said Mr. Waldruss finally.

"I thought he might be in the woods," James ventured hopelessly.

"I fear me he is," Mr. Waldruss said and needed to say no more.

That night James snuggled into his comfortable bed of feathers and again could not sleep for worry. He fretted half the night away, until suddenly he had a thought that sent him sitting bolt upright. *He's gone to the cave!* He was so sure of it he almost bounded down to awaken his master and drag him through the moonless night to rescue Davy. A sudden thought cautioned him. Why had Davy gone a long way off to an empty cave when he might have come to the welcoming comfort of the Waldruss home? He must have had a reason. Strange as was the idea of keeping a secret from his

master, James determined he had better find out first
before revealing anything to Mr. Waldruss.

He rushed about his chores that morning, and when
they started back to the house James said, "If you only
say so, I would spend the day looking for Davy."

"I say so, James," Mr. Waldruss answered kindly. "Perhaps you will have good luck. I would go with you,
but one of us must stay behind."

James was ashamed at the half-lie he had told, but
promised himself to make it good as soon as he had
the story from Davy. Accordingly, as soon as he had
finished breakfast he dressed his warmest and greased
his boots against the snow. Mrs. Waldruss packed a
wooden bucket with bread and a little firkin of raccoon
grease to salve Davy's wounds. She sought out an old
piece of homespun wool she had been saving to work
into a quilt, and this James wore over his head and
shoulders, hoping to wrap Davy in it. He carried his
knife as a weapon, for who knew what beasts were
abroad? Thus laden, he started off across the snow,
knowing he could reach the sugar clearing faster on
foot, going through the woods, than if he had a horse
to carry him along the path.

As he reached the first trees, he turned around and
saw Mr. Waldruss. His master was standing in the cold,
watching him and waving. James signalled in return,
then turned and plunged into the woods.

It was not an easy route, but it led directly to the
cave. When he reached the clearing and looked up at

the black mouth of the cave, his heart began to beat so fast he could hardly breathe. He stood motionless, scared. Now that he had reached journey's end, he was unwilling to try his idea. But finally the cold nipped him back into action. He climbed the little hill, and standing at the cave's opening, he called softly, "Davy?"

There was only silence. Again he called, louder. Again for a moment there was no sound. Then came a croaking reply, "James?"

James cried out his relief and entered the blackness and felt his way to Davy's side. He was chattering fever-

ishly: "How are you? Are you bad hurt? This part of
the cave is warm — it will be the saving of you!"

In the darkness Davy found his mittened hand and
said, more in a moan than in words, "Thank God you've
come."

It seemed hard for him to talk, but after a while
James was able to understand that Davy had been in
the cave since he'd run off. "It hurts to move, so mostly
I lie quiet. But I believe there are no bones broken.
And like an animal, I have heated my bit of cave with
the heat from my own body."

James put the woolen shawl on the floor of the cave
beside Davy. "Here is some warm wool, for when you
leave the cave. On it I place a knife, that you may not
be without some weapon. And now, if you can sit up, I
have bread for you and salve for your wounds."

Slowly Davy pulled himself up. Even in the dark
James could sense the pain and effort that went into it.
But then he was able to eat, wolfishly, pausing only once
to say, "Thank God for you, James Porter." Then, saying he felt better already, he added, "It was most brave
of you, James, to come to me thus. But what will you tell
Mr. Waldruss?"

It was a shock for James to realize that his fears were
confirmed. Davy expected him not to tell Mr. Waldruss.
He asked, "But won't you come home with me and be
cared for, Davy?" even though his heart sank with the
sure knowledge of what Davy's answer would be.

"Mr. Waldruss will only return me to Cotter," Davy

said, his voice sounding hard and angry. "It is the law, James. He has no choice."

"He will go to the Magistrate first," James protested, but Davy positively refused to return with him, and exacted a promise that James would not reveal the secret of the cave. James gave his promise readily. It was not until he was on his way home with his empty bucket that he realized that keeping his promise could involve him in lies to the master he loved so dearly. It seemed he must choose between on the one hand loyalty to his dearest friend and compassion for his present state and the evil condition of his servitude; and on the other hand, the honor of his relationship with his master.

He must not betray Davy, and he must not lie to Mr. Waldruss. His conflict so befuddled him that he lost his way. It was full dark before he found it again, bringing him home in a silent world of dark and shadows.

Mr. Waldruss stood outside, beside the window with the candle whose light had guided James home.

"Thank God you're safe," he said, and the simple words struck to James's heart like daggers. How could he lie to a master who was so unfailingly, so unceasingly kind? But how could he do other than lie, for his friend's sake? He knew that if Mr. Waldruss learned of Davy's whereabouts, he would feel duty-bound to reveal it to Mr. Cotter.

But his first words in reply could at least be true.

"I lost my way, sir," he said.

"I am glad you found it again, James, for I confess

I could sore spare you. You are as much to me as my own son by now, and I caution you as a father to take all good care of yourself."

Each word struck James with a new blow. They were the most precious words he had ever hoped to hear, and now they came at a time of betrayal.

Chapter 14

James Must Keep A Secret

"Now hark to me," Mr. Waldruss went on as they made their way to the house. He had taken the empty bucket from James's frozen hands. "You must search for Davy again, of course, but you must return by full daylight. And — " he swung the bucket, " — we must give you double food, in case you do find Davy. It is a sorry thing indeed to send you off with only enough food for yourself."

By only keeping silent James told his first lie, letting Mr. Waldruss believe he and not Davy had eaten. In truth he was famished. He had had little heart for eating for two days now, but his appetite had been fully restored by finding Davy. When Mrs. Waldruss set before him the meal she had kept hot he fell on it hungrily, barely pausing for breath.

When he had finished at last, Mrs. Waldruss asked suddenly, "And where is my good wool?"

James swallowed and replied, "I know where it is, ma'am. I will fetch it next time I pass that way." Before she could protest he added, "It is safe from the weather, in a cave where I rested for a while, and with it is the grease firkin."

"Where will you search tomorrow, James?" Mr. Waldruss asked as they sat by the fire, James toasting himself back to normal.

"I will enter the woods lower down," said James. Then, gathering all his courage, he asked, "But sir, what waits for Davy at the end? Only Mr. Cotter again?"

Mr. Waldruss nodded. "But I would go to the Magistrate before I go to Cotter, this time. If — when you find him, you must tell him that, poor lad." He sighed and went on quietly, "You must be prepared not to find him at all, until spring — when the snow melts."

James looked away from the picture his master had drawn, forgetting for the moment that he knew it was only a nightmare. Then, recollecting that he would need excuses for going daily to Davy, he said, "I will search for him every day, by your leave, sir."

"I will allow it for as long as you have heart for it," said Mr. Waldruss. "But you must come home by daylight. And James, if you do find him, do not conceal him. Tell me at once."

James had heard of the penalties for concealing an

escaped bondsman — a flogging at the very least await-
ed him. For himself, although he feared the punishment,
he could dare it. But would Mr. Waldruss, being his
master, be punished too even though innocent? He set
out to learn the truth and began a careful questioning:

"Sir, a person aiding an escaped bondsman — there
are severe penalties, are there not?"

Mr. Waldruss looked at him sharply but answered
only, "Make no mistake in it, James. The man who helps
is as liable as the man who runs away."

James sighed, then asked, "And if the man who helps
is himself a bondsman, would his master be liable?"

Mr. Waldruss again looked at James with penetrating
eyes. This time he answered only after a long pause.
"The master, if innocent, could not be held guilty. *But
James, it would go hard with his bondsman.*"

James recognized the warning, but rested content.
Since he would not involve his master, he could chance
what he liked for himself.

Every day James carried food to Davy. Of all the sac-
rifices he made for his friend, the one most painful was
in the matter of food. He must each day make it appear
that only one portion of food had been eaten. Thus he
would bring back half the food that he took away and
await his evening meal with hunger gnawing at him.

It was a long time before James ever saw Davy. It
was always in the warm dark of the cave that the two
were together. Davy said that he dragged himself out

of the cave occasionally, if only to get snow so it could melt in his mouth, but it chanced always to be at a time when James was not present. On a pleasant day when February began to look like melting into March, however, James came upon him leaning against the rocks by the cave. He ran to him joyfully, then fell back aghast. It seemed not to be Davy he saw, but an ugly stranger.

Although it was now weeks since his beating, there seemed no part of Davy that was not discolored still, or swollen, or festering. His face was a mass of healing cuts. His hands, where they were exposed, were a brownish purple.

Davy, observing James's dismay, smiled a little and said, "You should have seen me when he finished with me. I feared my blood would lay a clear track after me as I ran, it flowed so free. Only the covering snow saved me."

He held up his hands and looked at them. "I have forced myself to hold the knife and wood for whittling, else I would have lost my mind. But the pain has been great. My master Cotter spared me little."

Whenever he could, James advanced the idea of Davy's return to Mr. Waldruss, but Davy always refused flatly.

One day he sat and whittled away when James arrived, and on James bringing up the subject again, Davy said, "No, James, I have made up my mind what I must do. With the first warm weather I will make my way overland to Boston and ship on as a cabin boy. They

are not overparticular, those merchant captains, and will
be glad to take my word for it that I am a freeman.
It is not what I dreamed of, nor what I wish even now,
but anything will be better than Cotter again."

James could not blame Davy for wanting to escape
the five years of servitude that remained for him, if
that time must be served under Cotter. But to go as a
sailor! He was with Davy in saying it was not what he
would wish.

On this same day, a fine one, James returned home
to find Mr. Cotter at the house, sitting by the fire with
Mr. Waldruss. He had come to talk of the spring plowing, and as James entered he heard: "Then you will see
the Schutters, Waldruss?"

"Yes, tomorrow." Mr. Waldruss paused, then asked, "And how will you do without your boy?"

"Do without?" Mr. Cotter gave a short, contemptuous laugh. "He was a drag on me, eating more than his worth, and wearying me with his insolence. I wouldn't have him back now if he walked in that door and pleaded, the rascal."

"Would you not, indeed?" Mr. Waldruss asked mildly. "He seemed a famous worker to me."

Mr. Cotter fixed his eyes on James and said, "This is because you are satisfied with very little."

James bore no good will for Mr. Cotter and certainly less after that jibe. He stopped in the act of removing his jacket and started for the door, saying, "I will carry the water for the beasts, sir." He did not want to sit under the same roof with Mr. Cotter.

The next morning Mr. Waldruss, with cheerfulness seeming to burst out of every pore, a secretive kind of excitement twinkling out of his eyes, set out for Schutter's, saying, "I will call at Cotter's, too. I have dealings with him. Do not look for me till near dark."

Chapter 15

Mr. Waldruss Makes
A Purchase

Dark came and with it a full bright yellow moon, but there was no sign of Mr. Waldruss. As the moon rose higher, Mrs. Waldruss began to fret, saying, "I told him he should not go." James recalled hearing nothing of the sort, but did not mention it. "I told him I had a feeling — "

James, accustomed as he was to her feelings, could not this time laugh them away, for time passed and still his master did not come. He asked for and quickly received permission to go even as far as Cotter's to look for his master, but he had hardly gone two hundred yards in the slush before he heard a hail and saw a dark form near a clump of pines.

It was Mr. Waldruss. His horse had slipped in the

mud and thrown him, and he had lain where he was, unable to move from the pain in one leg.

"I fear me it is broken," he said huskily. "James, I am in great pain. You must leave me and go for help."

The good man fainted. James, after hovering over him helplessly for a moment, turned and raced back to the house as if he were on wings. By the barn he saw the horse, which had found its way back and seemed none the worse for the experience. But James did not stop to make sure. With Mrs. Waldruss' help he contrived a litter from two strong boughs and a sturdy linen cloth.

"We will bear him ourselves," Mrs. Waldruss said through her nervous tears. "Dear kind man, it is the good who suffer in this world."

James, who had had a bit of proof along these lines already, could only agree, and caution her against hurrying. "For indeed, ma'am, if you use all your strength in just getting to him, you will have none for the great trial of bringing him back."

Mr. Waldruss was still unconscious, which Mrs. Waldruss said was a great blessing. "For if we are to move him, no matter how gently, the pain would still be beyond bearing."

It was a slow trip back indeed, for Mr. Waldruss was a heavy man. James joined Mrs. Waldruss in gratitude that his master was unconscious. He could not have borne to see more suffering.

Once he was safely in the house, James set out on the horse for Cousin Beadle. It had been decided to

ask him to go into Boston, there to find Dr. Waite and
bring him back. It being bright moonlight, Cousin Beadle could set out at once if he would.

The ride through the woods was eerie in the white
light of the moon. James sat the horse and looked
straight forward, terrified of what lay ready to spring at
him from his right or left. Here in the woods the snow
still lay soft but unmelted, impeding the horse's prog-
ress but at least not tricking him into another fall. There
were strange sounds to be heard above the clip-clop of

his horse's hoofs, strange cries as forest animals were
disturbed in their rest by the noise of his passing,
screams that seemed unearthly as they came from one
nocturnal beast or another. James drew tight in on himself, cowering on the horse, his fear growing with each
hoofbeat. And yet he knew all the time he was in no real
danger and was ashamed of fears that were for himself
alone and not for the good man at home who would
awaken only to pain.

The ride to Cousin Beadle's took too long, as even a
minute might be too long; but once there, and once
having shouted and banged the family awake, James was
welcomed in with kindness and sympathy.

"Of course, I'll go, and at once," said Cousin Beadle.
"And will you come with me?"

James wanted to go with him, or anywhere, rather
than take the terrifying ride back through the woods;
but he knew he would be needed at home, and so he
refused. He wished he could be brave as Davy would
certainly have been. He could not fancy Davy in terror of
a night ride through the woods. Yet terror or not, he
must go back the way he came. Having seen Cousin
Beadle on his way to the shallop, he mounted again
and started back.

He was more prepared now. It was not that he was
less afraid but rather that he knew his fear was mainly
unreasonable. He could take even the moon swinging
low just before dawn so that the last few minutes in
the woods were very dark, for he could tell himself,

soon I will be in the clear. And then he was in the clear, and in the first rays of the rising sun he could see the house, a candle in the window for him, and he thought suddenly, ah, poor Mr. Waldruss! It is a strange way I am made, he told himself, ashamed again. I am a fearful, forgetful boy, and I must try to do better.

Mr. Waldruss was awake and in great pain. He looked briefly relieved when James told him that Cousin Beadle was on the way, but he did not speak except once, when the sun was high, to ask, "James, how is the wind?"

James ran outside and let the wind blow into his face, then back to report eagerly, "A brisk wind, sir, and just now coming from the north."

"Thank God," Mr. Waldruss breathed, and even the littlest girls knew enough to echo the prayer. A good strong wind would bring Cousin Beadle and his shallop back the quicker, and with him the physician.

By nightfall the worst was over. Dr. Waite came in, looking around at the house and furnishings as if he disapproved of what he saw. He went to Mr. Waldruss and lightly touched the swollen leg. He observed it, walked about it as if it were a curiosity. Then he sent Cousin Beadle and James for wood to make splints, and when they brought in a piece of maple that Mr. Waldruss himself had sawed into a plank, he used an ax with such sureness that it was a joy to watch.

When the plank had been chopped into pieces of the right size, Cousin Beadle and James held Mr. Waldruss down, Mr. Waldruss gritted his teeth, and the job was done. The worst of the pain eased almost at once, but of course it would be many a weary week before Mr. Waldruss would be able to walk.

Dr. Waite was to go back to Boston with Cousin Beadle, but before he left Mr. Waldruss asked, "How may I pay you, sir?"

"Know you that I work only for cash," Dr. Waite said. "None of your barter for me."

"But do you have enough fresh eggs in the city, sir?" Mrs. Waldruss asked. "A few hens, so little care they are, would provide you with — "

"Hard cash — and English money only," Dr. Waite said.

"I have only seven shillings to my name," Mr. Waldruss said. "But if that is not enough I will beg you to let my Cousin Beadle deliver what foodstuffs you will feel fair when he takes you back."

Dr. Waite hesitated, then shrugged and said, "I will not take your last shilling. Give me six, and call it even."

Mrs. Waldruss brought the pewter cup, and Mr. Waldruss paid out the six shillings. Cousin Beadle and the doctor departed.

"You had a pound more yesterday," Mrs. Waldruss said as soon as the men had left. "How is it now we are left with only a shilling?"

"Ah, yes!" Mr. Waldruss was cheerful now, in spite of what he had been through. "That pound! I made an investment with that pound."

"An investment!" Mrs. Waldruss said in tones of displeasure. "I hope you are not thinking of the rum trade. I would never like that."

"No, no, it is something very different. I have been much troubled by James's seeking day after day for his friend. I was fearful — well, what I have done is buy Davy's time for one pound."

"He is raving," Mrs. Waldruss said in great alarm. "Hear him talk so wild! Talking of buying a runaway who can't be found."

"As to that, Cotter felt exactly like you. He thought me a fool to pay the pound, because Cotter believes the boy is dead. I told him I was sure Davy was safe somewhere or other and would turn up. Cotter took my money and called me a fool. But he took my money first. Well, James, I own your friend now, and I only pray he will not turn up too soon, else Cotter will call me a thief."

He grew very serious now and went on, "The penalty for helping an escaped bondsman is so severe that I felt I must protect you in case you were tempted to help Davy. And Cotter is so sure the boy is dead, I may have thrown my pound away. He must have beaten him sore to be so sure he is dead, don't you agree?"

James gulped and answered, "Yes, sir, he — must."

"And Davy would have great need of a friend, if that be so."

"Yes, sir, he — would."

"Then if *in a few weeks* you should find him, tell him to come home."

James had needed no further proof of his master's kindness, but here it was again!

"There might be some little trickery in my transaction," Mr. Waldruss mused. "But I have thought long on it, and I am sure it is right to rescue a human soul by whatever means come to hand."

"I never thought you a chatterbox," Mrs. Waldruss said, but looking very proud, as if she understood nothing he had said but knew him as a man to be admired. "Now, save your breath to cool your porridge, do."

James was more open now in requesting food for Davy, although he still pretended he was going to seek him. He packed a supply to last for a few days and ran jubilantly to tell Davy the news. The two boys laughed and cried together and agreed on the wait of three weeks that Mr. Waldruss had suggested before Davy came home.

"Home," Davy repeated softly. And then, "How strangely it has turned out, James. I was going to care for you!"

But by the time only three days had passed, their plans came to nothing. Mr. Waldruss, while his leg seemed to be going on well, had begun to burn with a fever, and none of Mrs. Waldruss' simples seemed to help. She might dose him with a brew of herbs, and yet he seemed warmer to the touch. She might lay upon his forehead a mixture of mutton fat and aromatic leaves, and still he burned.

At the end of a whole day of watching such trials and

failures, James went to the barn to see to the beasts, for naturally all the chores fell on him now. He hoped that the activity of his body might somehow ease the anxiety of his mind. There was no denying Mr. Waldruss was very sick. He lay quiet and silent, a strange thing for a man who was such a great talker. James felt such fear as he had never known in a whole fear-filled lifetime. Oh, what shall I do if he goes? he asked himself and buried his face in the horse's mane.

It was thus that Mrs. Waldruss found him.

"Ah, poor James," she said and then gave a quick sob. "James, you must get Cousin Beadle to go again for Dr. Waite."

"But ma'am, he comes only for cash," James reminded her fearfully. "Ma'am, what are we to do?"

She stood staring at him in a terror of her own, then said, "I will look for everything we own that can be turned into cash." She sighed. "It will be a sorry lot."

She hastened back to the house. When James returned she and the girls had set on the table the pewter cups and pitcher and the single shilling they had left. Ranged about nearby were all her tubs and firkins and wooden bowls.

"Ma'am, you won't be able to mix bread or milk cows," James said. "Ma'am, your fear for your husband blinds you. This is not sensible."

"Without my good man nothing will matter," Mrs. Waldruss said sadly, and James mourned with her.

There was not enough there, all having been used be-

fore, to bring Dr. Waite out again — and it would leave
them at a great disadvantage. For how could they milk
a cow without a bucket for the milk? And how could
Mrs. Waldruss mix her delicious bread with no bowl?
And the butter firkin? And the wooden mixing knife?

He suddenly felt the need of advice and comfort,
and all he could think of was Davy, his dear friend and
now his brother servant.

"I'm off for Cousin Beadle's," he said. "But first I must
consult with Davy."

There was a surprised outcry from Mrs. Waldruss and
Elizabeth and Hitty.

"Bless my soul!" Mrs. Waldruss exclaimed. "Then you
know where he is to be found?"

"Yes, ma'am," James said, and sped from the house
as she called more questions after him.

Chapter 16

Davy Solves A Problem

In the fading afternoon James went racing fleetly through the woods to the sugar clearing, too frightened now for his master to have room for any other fears.

"Davy, what are we to do?"

He had prayed Davy would have an answer, and Davy did! He went into the cave and brought forth the accumulation he had whittled over the idle weeks. There were mixing spoons and ladles and a wooden knife that he said would do well for cutting butter. He had wooden pegs to use for nails and twig whistles for the children.

"These will bring cash for our master!" he said proudly and taking the woolen shawl wrapped them into it.

"But who will sell them?" James asked. "Cousin Beadle is a rough fisherman, a timid man in the way of business if ever there was one. And though it would not be easy, I could overcome my own shyness and sell in the streets of Boston if I could leave Mrs. Waldruss now. But she needs me. Busy as she is with her poor husband, she would have to let the beasts die of thirst."

"Then I will go," said Davy, drawing himself up and looking a proud, handsome youth in spite of the scars that still remained. "I will hawk them from street to street. I will hawk them on the wharves. I will sell each thing for the best price and earn a pound or more. Take me to Cousin Beadle, and I will go with him to Boston."

The two boys, carrying their burden of woodenware between them, ran fleetly through the woods until they reached the barn. Here James left Davy and ran to tell the Waldrusses that they were on their way and what their plans were.

"God will help us," Mrs. Waldruss said pathetically. "I have tried a brew of sassafras to no avail. We must have the doctor."

James and Davy sprang onto the horse, Davy in the saddle, James before him, and in front of all the bundle of woodenware.

Cousin Beadle was again obliging and concerned, and again James must ride home through the woods alone. But now he was not troubled by childish fears. He heard the screeches of the owl, the howls of the animals, as if in a dream. All he thought of was reaching home to take up a vigil at his master's bedside.

"You must sleep, ma'am," he said. "I will stay here where I can spring to his service at a moment's notice."

"You are a good boy, James," Mrs. Waldruss said. She was exhausted and climbed upstairs to lie down on the children's bed. James poked up the fire and added a log. Mr. Waldruss heard him and said petulantly, as unlike himself as any invalid could be, "You waste wood, James."

"Yes, and I'd waste more to have you warm, sir," James said firmly, taking a strong tone he had never used before. "I will care for you until the doctor comes."

He marvelled at himself for talking so but decided that love and fear make powerful bedfellows. He did not regret his words, especially when Mr. Waldruss drifted back into sleep, however fitful it might be.

James meant to sleep. He meant to stretch out by the fire and sleep while his master slept, but he found himself unable to shut his eyes. Dear sir, he found himself thinking, dear master, hold on, hold on. When his master awakened, muttering and talking strangely, James wrung a piece of linen out of cold water and put it to the burning head.

The cold seemed to shock his master awake. He looked intelligently at James.

"I'm bad sick, am I, James?" he asked.

"I cannot lie to you, sir," James said. "And still it is only a fever. But Dr. Waite will cure it."

"Dr. Waite asks for cash," Mr. Waldruss cried out in alarm.

"Indeed, and he'll get it," James said, and told how Davy was going to achieve it. "Indeed, sir, you have no need to worry about money."

"Have I not, then?" Mr. Waldruss said, with a hint of his old wit. "It'll be the first time, if it be so."

Now he went back into his feverishness, and no change of the cold linen helped. At dawn Mrs. Waldruss joined James and wept silently at the sight of her husband so sick. She still had a thought for James and whispered, "Do you now go and have some sleep, boy."

But Davy went instead to the barn and busied himself all that day until, as the sun began to sink, he thought, surely they will come before the moon rises.

He was not wrong. He thought, and learned it to be true later, that Davy had so badgered Dr. Waite that the poor man had no choice but to embark, even though it was long past midday before Davy had sold all his wares.

They came into the house, an anxious Cousin Beadle with them. Davy brought in hope with his confident smile, in the way he slapped his pocket and winked at James, in the way he said so assuredly, "We've brought the best man for the job. Now soon all will be well."

Dr. Waite had his secret medicinal draughts with him, and his leeches and his poultices. Davy whispered to James, "We'll never know if 'twas nature pulling the master through, or the doctor's doses," but however it might be, the draught seemed to quiet Mr. Waldruss, and the poultices seemed to sooth, and the leeches could do no harm. By nightfall he was cooler, and Dr. Waite said he would now soon be cured of his fever. When Dr. Waite left, it was with a silver pound from Davy, who handed it over negligently, as if there were more where that came from.

After Dr. Waite and Cousin Beadle left and the family clustered around the bed, Mr. Waldruss was able to smile at them all. He almost laughed at the ridiculous ceremony Davy made of dropping his three remaining pennies into the pewter mug.

Mr. Waldruss did mend quickly. Each day saw him stronger, brighter. His clever cheerfulness returned, and life in the family resumed its brisk, happy way. In addition there was the wonderful gaiety that Davy brought into the house. His natural assurance had returned now

that he was safely Mr. Waldruss' servant. He helped
them all.

When Mr. Waldruss began to worry about the plowing, Davy said, "Rest easy, sir. James and I will do your
part. Remember I had a master who taught me to do
the work of two men."

When Mrs. Waldruss, in her way, worried about
stretching bedding far enough to warm both boys, he
said gaily, "But ma'am, summer will soon be here. By
next fall we will have plucked enough geese for a dozen
quilts."

He was so full of determined hopefulness that they
all caught hope from him.

Chapter 17

Like Brothers

Now came the time for plowing.

James's fear of Cotter's wrath was great. What might he not do on seeing Davy alive and strong as ever? True, Mr. Waldruss had tried to protect Davy. He had sent James to Schutter's to ask the German to visit him. When the good-natured Schutter came, Mr. Waldruss explained how he came to be Davy's master and showed the paper that proved it. He bade Davy show the healing lash marks. Schutter, who had added many more words to his English in the years that had passed, said, "Bad, very bad, ah, poor boy." When he left it was with a promise to keep Cotter from injuring Davy again.

"Now we have done all we can, boys. Have a civil

153

tongue for Cotter. Remember he is a harsh man with a
quick temper, and guard yourselves, for I will not be
with you. I fear Cotter bears me no love for buying
Davy. It is the habit of men to be angry where they
feel themselves to be wrong, and in his mind he has
cheated me of a pound sterling by selling me a boy he
believes dead." He hesitated and added wryly, "I can
judge his wrath when he learns the truth. His first sight
of Davy will surely enrage him." Again he paused, and
this time sighed. "I dearly wish we did not need Cotter
and his oxen."

But need him they did, and although James trembled
and even Davy seemed unable to find a hearty or amus-
ing word to wipe the threat of Cotter away, the two
boys had to make ready for the first day's work.

Schutter and his sons had cleared more land, and
since his would again be the hardest fields, they were
to meet first at his barn. When James opened his eyes
in the dark before the sun rose, he could tell from the
freshness in the air that the day would dawn clear and
dry, though he had prayed for rain. He hesitated only a
moment, his fear holding him, but there was no escap-
ing it. The day had come, and he and Davy alone must
do their master's work. They must brave Mr. Cotter's ire
to do it.

He shook Davy gently awake, and the two boys went
quietly down the ladder, hoping not to disturb Mr. Waldruss. Mrs. Waldruss slept soundly on her pallet on the
floor, and the boys would have gone on tiptoe to the

door but that in the dimness Mr. Waldruss' voice, pitched
very low, commanded them to wait.

"It is the first time in thirty years I have not been in
the fields at the first turning of the earth," he said, not
sadly, for that was not his way, but with real regret.
"But boys, do not leave without food. Your mistress is
worn out with caring for me. We will not wake her to
cook porridge, but fill yourselves up with milk and
bread. The sun will be high before you taste Mrs. Schutter's good food."

Davy went in his nimble way to fetch the milk from
the cold corner, and James at his more cautious pace to
get the bread. They ate and drank in the quiet dimness,
not speaking. When they were finished they whispered,
"Good-bye, sir," and got his "God bless you both," in
return.

They shut the door behind them and went to the
barn for the oxen. There began to be a faint glow in
the sky as they travelled. James thought, it will be a
fine day, but it will be ruined for me by my fear of
Cotter.

"Are you afraid of Cotter, Davy?" he asked finally.

"I can't say I am not," Davy replied. "He is a man
of terrible rages."

This cast James down more than ever. If even Davy
was afraid, who knew what might happen?

The sun was not full up when they came to Schutter's. Although they could see candles burning within,
they did not make their presence known for fear of

seeming to hurry the German family. They left the oxen near the barn and walked quietly toward the house, prepared to wait patiently outside. Rounding a corner, they came without warning upon the Cotters.

There stood Catto, Simon — and Mr. Cotter! It was Catto who gasped out, "Davy! Alive! God be praised!"

"Father, here is your bondsman once more," Simon said. He was poised and greedy for his father to strike the first blow. And indeed Mr. Cotter seemed about to satisfy him. His face was turning red with rage, his fist was half upraised.

James turned helplessly to Davy, who stood very still, his head held high as if not deigning to shrink. Speak,

run, cry out, James pleaded inwardly, but Davy only stood as if awaiting the first blow.

"Mr. Cotter!" James called out suddenly over the terror that possessed him. "Mr. Cotter, sir!"

The man turned slowly and stared at James. "You, boy, what do you want?"

"My master has sent both his boys, sir, to replace him and do his share of the work. My master wishes me to remind you that Davy is now his. He has Davy's paper with your signature. My master says it will go hard indeed with anyone who molests his servants. My master is a large man. As soon as he can walk again he will have vengeance on the first man who dares strike a servant of his."

Mr. Cotter stood with his arm upraised for a moment longer, then dropped it. He turned back to look at Davy.

"He was no bargain. Waldruss is welcome to the rogue," he muttered.

The next instant the Schutters joined them. Mr. Schutter looked sharply from Mr. Cotter to Davy.

"All ready?" he asked in his accented English.

Cotter glared once more at Davy, but nothing more was said. They went for the oxen.

When the first clear cry to the team came ringing through the fresh spring dawn, James's heart gave a grateful thump, and he said in an undertone to Davy, "You are safe!"

"I am, and by your work. James, I thought you afraid of Mr. Cotter?"

"Indeed, and I was."

"Ah, that was courage, then! To rise over your fear
that way! You are a brave lad, James!"

Brave? James worked with a new will, elated at
the word. He could see what Davy meant. Where was
the courage in a deed that took no courage? He thought
of all the times he had been afraid and had yet pro-
ceeded to do the very thing he feared. He realized now
that it was not the fear that mattered, but the over-
coming of it. It was in the doing of the deed in spite
of fear that courage was tested. He was brave. Davy had
said so, and he knew it was true.

He and Davy worked on side by side all that day,
as if it were a pattern for all the days to follow. Their
joy and comfort in one another increased steadily as
their position in the Waldruss family became daily more
like sons to the good man who was their master.

Both boys could say that their best hopes on the ship
coming out to America were not as great as the reality
of their lives in the new country.